CUBA

GOOD STORIES REVEAL as much, or more, about a locale as any map or guidebook. Whereabouts Press is dedicated to publishing books that will enlighten a traveler to the soul of a place. By bringing a country's stories to the English-speaking reader, we hope to convey its culture through literature. Books from Whereabouts Press are essential companions for the curious traveler, and for the person who appreciates how fine writing enhances one's experiences in the world.

"Coming newly into Spanish, I lacked two essentials —a childhood in the language, which I could never acquire, and a sense of its literature, which I could."

—Alastair Reid, *Whereabouts: Notes on Being a Foreigner*

CUBA

A TRAVELER'S LITERARY COMPANION

EDITED AND WITH A PREFACE BY
ANN LOUISE BARDACH

WHEREABOUTS PRESS
BERKELEY, CALIFORNIA

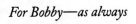

For Bobby—as always

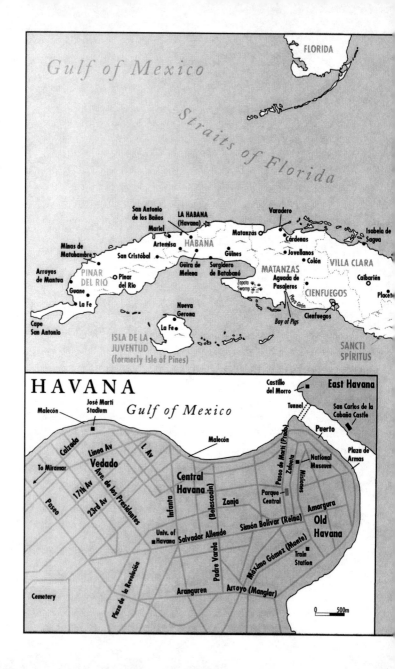

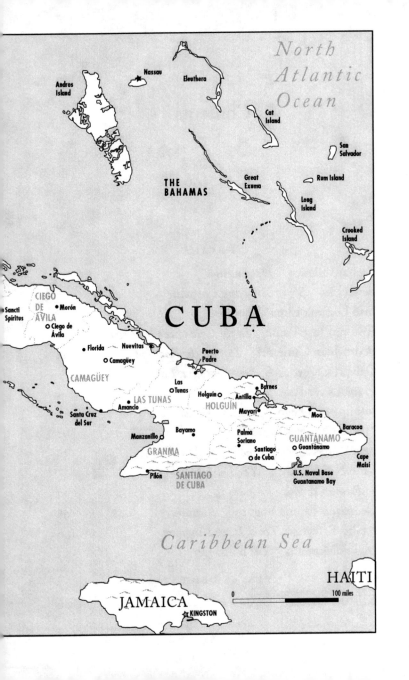

Contents

Preface

Ann Louise Bardach

In 1960, thunderstruck by the notion of vanquishing a 30 percent illiteracy rate, Fidel Castro ordered thousands of educated urbanites into the countryside to teach the ABCs to any *campesino* they happened upon. The success of the Literacy Brigades (Cuba not only leads Latin America in literacy rates, it has surpassed the United States) is the most significant and arguably sole surviving "triumph of the Revolution." Forty years later, the Maximum Leader decided that Cubans should be trilingual and inaugurated the University for All, which teaches English and French—among other subjects—daily on television. But it is one of the richer ironies of Castro's island fiefdom that every Cuban seems to have a color TV but nothing to read. Owing to decades of stupefying mismanagement, many of its hypereducated population have no books, no paper, and no pens.

Hence, in 1996, when a rare printing (10,000 copies) of an anthology of short stories by women writers titled *Estatuas de Sal* (Pillars of Salt) appeared, it sold out in less than two weeks. A second printing of 10,000 sold out even faster. Black market vendors were asking $10.00 (roughly two months' wages for the average Cuban) per copy for the book—and getting it. But what was most striking about this collection was its casual criticism of the government. Some of its stories were overtly dissident, others gently mocking, but almost all were layered with the battle fatigue of life in Cuba today.

"Who would have thought that after twenty plus years of work and with a university degree, I'd have to stand here on this corner selling my monthly cigarettes?" groans the smart-ass narrator of Josefina de Diego's "Internal Monologue on a Corner in Havana," one of the two selections included in this collection from that watershed anthology. De Diego goes on to mock the government's penchant for initializing all its bureaucracies. "CADECA . . . Such an ugly acronym, they really outdid themselves this time. There are other terrible, historic ones like CONACA or ECOA, but this one is the worst." Even her reminisces of "the good old days," prompt a sour memory. "The important thing is attitude, *companera*," she is reminded when she complains of being unable to make ends meet. Hungry for food and desperate for a smoke, she ponders the central dilemma of Cuba's Special Period, the official euphemism for the years of deprivation that followed in the wake of the Russian pullout of Cuba: "To smoke or eat, that is the question."

Pillars of Salt was notable for its inclusion of exile writers such as Ruth Behar, Uva de Aragón, Mayra Montero, and Achy Obejas. In Obejas's short story, "We Came All the Way from Cuba So You Could Dress Like This?" which chronicles her family's awkward adaptation into the American mainstream, the portrait of her late father is unforgettable: On the day that Teófilo Stevenson, the great Cuban boxer, triumphs at the Olympics, her father leaps from his easy chair in front of the TV and cheers—his rancorous heartbreak and exile politics momentarily stilled. And during the medal ceremony and the playing of the Cuban national anthem he "will stand up in Miami and cover his heart with his palm just like Fidel, watching on his own TV in Havana."

My introduction to Cuban literature came through a brief but cherished friendship with the late esteemed critic, José Rodríguez Feo, whose influence spanned fifty years. In addition to his considerable gifts as an essayist, translator, and critic, he was enormously rich at one time. A former aristocrat and libertine at the hub of the gay intelligentsia, Rodríguez Feo emerged as the Cuban Maecenas, as Guillermo Cabrera Infante dubbed him, and unstintingly bankrolled Havana's literati. As the postwar dean of Cuban letters, he encouraged, mentored, fed, and clothed writers and artists—from Virgilio Piñera to Reinaldo Arenas to Abilio Estévez—for four decades.

Rodríguez Feo was sent to Choate and Harvard where he studied American literature and later translated his two literary loves, T. S. Eliot and Wallace Stevens. "One semester at Harvard in 1939, I got a dividend check from my uncle's sugar mill for $70,000," he said, adding with a dry smile, "which was quite a bit of money back then." During his prep school days at Choate, he recalled, "I wrote an essay about the workers putting a sugar mill on fire in protest. I don't know how it came to me." In the 1940s, he cofounded with his close friend, José Lezama Lima, *Orígenes*, the pioneering literary journal of Cuba that published the work of both established and emerging writers, artists, and poets. Later in collaboration with Virgilio Piñera, he underwrote and edited *Ciclón*, an avant-garde literary review.

Over several afternoons, Rodríguez Feo, known to all as

Pepe, regaled me with stories from the late 1950s when revolutionary fever was so pitched "that even my uncle, the
sugar baron, gave money to Fidel. And when Fidel came to
power he made my cousin, Alberto, the head of the Sugar
Institute. In 1959, my uncle said publicly that the Revolution was abandoning its principles and that the businessmen would be betrayed." Virtually all of Rodríguez Feo's
family left Cuba, but he neither believed nor cared about
his uncle's prophecy. He stayed behind, turned over his
family's properties to the Revolution and signed up for the
Literacy Brigades.

But his revolutionary ardor was sorely tested in the late
1960s and early 1970s. Unlike Cuba's Film Institute or the
National Ballet of Cuba, the Writers Union (UNEAC) had
no guardian angels, and getting published was the preserve
of the ideologically pure. In 1971 State Security officials
arrested the brilliant poet Heberto Padilla, a hard-drinking
bear of a man, who had been critical of the government in
his conversations and his work. Thirty-eight days after his
arrest, an ashen Padilla was ushered into UNEAC by State
Security agents where he confessed his sins. "He told everyone how he thought the Revolution was really beautiful,"
said Rodríguez Feo who witnessed Padilla denounce his
friends as counterrevolutionaries, who, in turn, rushed forward to confess their subversive ways. Following a ten-year
international lobbying campaign, Padilla was allowed to
leave Cuba in 1981.

By the time I met Pepe in 1993, there wasn't much love
left in his love-hate relationship with the Revolution and
Fidel Castro. The three flights of stairs leading to his small
apartment in Vedado were unlit and smelled of urine. It was

the height of the Special Period and Havana reminded me of my student days in New York City during the garbage strike with trash piled six feet high in the streets. When I asked where all his fine belongings had gone, he nodded to a bookcase holding a bound set of *Orígenes* and said, "These are all that matter. This is what I am most proud of." When his other guests, bantering about Fidel Castro, drifted out of the room, Pepe leaned in close to me and whispered hoarsely. "He destroyed this country because of his pride," he said. "And that's a monster."

"It wasn't the censorship that was so terrible," Pepe told me a month before he died of cancer in 1994. "The self-censorship was worse." Still he had no regrets. "I could not have lived in exile," he said with a shrug, adding that few Cuban writers could. He pointed out that Padilla's finest work had been written in Cuba. "He never wrote like that again," he said. His lack of bitterness was puzzling. But Pepe simply wagged his finger, Cuban style, in front of his face. He had been rich, he had been broke, he had known the very finest minds of several generations, and the very worst. It had been an adventure. "More interesting than living in Miami," he said, with a quick roll of the eyes.

Unfortunately, Pepe did not get to see the window of opportunity flutter open again as it did in the late 1990s. The dramatic debut in 2000 of Pedro Juan Gutiérrez's *Dirty Havana Trilogy*, unthinkable even five years earlier, flabbergasted many with its audacious nihilism. But the rules had changed, as they are wont to do in Cuba with the exception of one: "Inside the Revolution, anything; outside the Revolution, nothing." And Gutiérrez's corrosive portrait of magnificent Havana as a fetid ecosystem of godless desperados pushed the limits of the official mantra to the maximum.

The fact that Gutiérrez is able to live in Cuba and is not in jail after penning such a derisive work speaks to one of the mysteries and secrets of the forty-two-year-old endurance run of Fidel Castro. But in the wake of the Special Period and the crumbling of the CDR's (Committees to Defend the Revolution), complaining is okay, but doing something about it—like organizing a demonstration—is not. And Cubans have made the complaint—the safety valve of the Revolution—into an art form. Even Cuba's Minister of Culture, writer Abel Prieto, has published his own novel, *El Vuelo del Gato* (The Flight of the Cat), which takes its share of elliptical swipes at the Cuban Revolution.

Still Gutiérrez hammers the complaint to the wall. *Trilogy* follows the daily scramblings of its narrator Pedro Juan, the baddest, coolest dude on the Malecón, who, like the author, is a former journalist, street vendor, scammer, and hustler. Gutiérrez vividly recreates the claustrophobic squalor of Havana's underbelly with ultraviolet cameos of its lost souls and gritty survivors. Gutiérrez is most reminiscent of Zoé Valdés who left Cuba in the late 1990s. Both writers mine Cuban street life and together they have forged a Cuban subgenre that could well be called "I'm writing as dirty as I can."

While it is largely true that sex—even infidelity—is the national sport of Cuba, Gutiérrez's sex is always detached and devoid of love. Sex is a divertissement, a respite from boredom, a balm against feeling, a cheap opiate. What's unsaid is that sex in Cuba is the one zone of complete unfettered freedom, where rebellion and dissidence is tolerated.

Certainly there is a tradition of dirty writing in Cuba. Most notable is chapter eight of José Lezama Lima's baroque masterpiece *Paradiso,* whose byzantine diction evokes Fitzgerald's immodest appraisal of his own work, "blankets of beautiful prose." Gutiérrez even outdoes Reinaldo Arenas's famed libidity. In the parlance of the recovery movement, Pedro Juan is a hopeless sex addict with palpable self-loathing. "My heart is hard now, and the only feeling I have for women is in my erections."

Abilio Estévez's *Thine Is the Kingdom* lies at the opposite end of the literary spectrum. Estévez, who lives in Havana, is an interesting counterpart to exile writer Ernesto Mestre's equally inspired and masterful novel *The Lazarus Rumba.* Whereas Gutiérrez is rather self-consciously the Cuban descendant of Bukowski and Genet, Estévez's ancestor is Virgilio Piñera, the lyrical Cuban master: harassed during his life for his homosexuality, but *rehabilitated* and revered in Cuba today. *Kingdom* is dedicated to Piñera who died in 1979.

Set on the eve of the Cuban Revolution in a once stately, now decaying Havana mansion called the Island, Estévez's fable is peopled with a troop of disparate eccentrics. "Like any Cubans," the narrator tells us halfway through his tale, "the characters in this book have never learned to live alone. Cubans don't want to know that men are all alone in the world." Later, he chastises them: "You don't have exclusive rights to human suffering; it's characterized all Cuban literature, as you know."

I have sought to make this anthology as inclusive and diverse as possible: representing the old masters, the young Turks, exiles, residents, *mujeriegos* (skirt chasers), women, and gay men. Estévez, Gutiérrez, Valdés, de Diego, Ponte,

Alegría Nuñez, Padura Fuentes, and Senel Paz are Cuba's baby boomers, their childhoods forged in the revolutionary culture of the preposterous New Man, their teen years bearing witness to the flight of thousands of Cubans during *Mariel,* and later, the death of the Soviet-financed welfare state. Moreover, they confront the staggering literary legacy of such postwar giants as José Lezama Lima, Virgilio Piñera, Severo Sarduy, Alejo Carpentier, and others. Rarely, if ever, is there mention of the aging *barbudo* warrior partial to olive-green fatigues. Yet for all of Cuba's postwar writers, Fidel Castro and his forty-two-year-old social experiment is the unidentified elephant in the room.

Inexplicably and regrettably, the Cuban government denied us permission to reprint stories of Piñera and Carpentier in this collection. On the other side of the great mad overcaffeinated Cuban divide, some exile writers refused to be in a collection that includes writers still living in Cuba. To illuminate this highbrow telenovela and explicate Cuban character, we rely on the lucid insights of Luis Aguilar Leon's monograph *The Prophet.*

Still, we are able to publish in English for the first time Alfonso Hernández Catá's "Don Cayetano," the story of a rancher who, on the eve of selling his land, meets the ghost of José Martí, Cuba's independence hero and poet. The singularly gifted and tormented Calvert Casey, who took his own life in 1969, contributes "My Aunt Leocadia, Love, and the Lower Paleolithic," an exquisite tale of reminiscence. The brilliant hyperbolic imagination of Reinaldo Arenas finds eloquence and chilling fury in an excerpt from his novella, *Old Rosa.* Other classics include an excerpt from the masterful Lino Novás Calvo's "The Dark Night of

Ramón Yendía," a feverish tale of the relentless hunt for a man suspected of being on the wrong side of the political divide. Though written in the early 1940s, it is a timeless parable for a country that has never known democracy. Also, excerpted is Senel Paz's modern classic, *The Wolf, the Woods and the New Man*— which was translated into the Academy Award–nominated film, *Strawberry and Chocolate*.

From the exile front, I've included Cristina Garcia's sublime "Ocean Blue," excerpted work from Pablo Medina, Ana Menéndez, Richard Blanco, and the extraordinary Mayra Montero. A story by Uva de Aragón, "Not the Truth, Not a Lie," is published here for the first time. Of course, there are dozens of writers who should have been included in this collection but who are the unintended victims of space, copyrights snafus, and inevitably, politics.

One may well ask how a small Caribbean country produces such a diverse harvest of world-class writers. Undoubtedly it must be the Cuban love of the word, the passion for speech. "If there is anything common to all Cubans it is the fact that we talk a lot," notes the Cuban writer René Vásquez Díaz. "We need to have noise, the endless bubbling of words because we have to fill the silence with anything, at any cost. . . . Silence is the enemy of the Cubans. When we have nothing to say, we sing. . . . We use language against silence, that is, against death."

JANUARY 2002

Havanasis

Richard Blanco

IN THE BEGINNING, before God created Cuba, the earth was chaos, empty of form and without music. The spirit of God stirred over the dark tropical waters and God said, "Let there be music." And a soft conga began a one-two beat in the background of the chaos.

Then God called up *Yemayá* and said, "Let the waters under heaven amass together and let dry land appear." It was done. God called the fertile red earth Cuba and the massed waters the Caribbean. And God saw this was good, tapping his foot to the conga beat.

Then God said, "Let the earth sprout *papaya* and *coco* and white *coco* flesh; *malanga* roots and mangos in all shades of gold and amber; let there be *tabaco* and *café* and sugar for the *café*; let there be rum; let there be waving plantains and *guayabas* and everything tropical-like." God saw this was good, then fashioned palm trees—His pièce de résistance.

Then God said, "Let there be a moon and stars to light the nights over the Club Tropicana, and a sun for the 365 days of the year." God saw that this was good; He called the night nightlife, the day He called paradise.

Then God said, "Let there be fish and fowl of every kind." And there was spicy shrimp *enchilado*, chicken *fric-*

asé, codfish *bacalao,* and fritters. But He wanted something more exciting and said, Enough. Let there be pork." And there was pork—deep fried, whole roasted, pork rinds, and sausage. He fashioned goats, used their skins for bongos and *batús;* he made *claves* and *maracas* and every kind of percussion instrument known to man.

Then out of a red lump of clay, God made a Taino and set him in a city He called *Habana.* Then He said, "It is not good that Taino be alone. Let me make him helpmates." And so God created the *mulata* to dance *guaguancó* and *son* with Taino; the *guajiro* to cultivate his land and his folklore, *Cachita* the sorceress to strike the rhythm of his music, and a poet to work the verses of their paradise.

God gave them dominion over all the creatures and musical instruments and said unto them, "Be fruitful and multiply, eat pork, drink rum, make music, and dance." On the seventh day, God rested from the labors of His creation. He smiled upon the celebration and listened to their music.

Strawberry and Chocolate

Senel Paz

FOR THE LEZAMA LIMA LUNCH he made me wear a shirt and tie. Bruno lent me one, and forced ten pesos on me as well, thinking that I was taking a girl out to the Tropicana. The exceptional quality of a lunch, as I later discovered Lezama himself wrote in *Paradiso*, springs from its embroidered tablecloth that isn't red or white but cream to contrast with the gleaming white enamel of the dinner service edged in tawny green. Diego took the lid off the soup tureen, where a thick plantain soup was steaming. "I wanted to rejuvenate you," he said smiling mysteriously, "by taking you back to your early childhood, so that's why I've added a little tapioca to the soup . . ." "And what's that?" "Yucca my baby, but don't interrupt me. I've floated some sweet corn on top, there are just so many things we liked as kids that we've never enjoyed since. But don't worry, it's not the so-called Wild West soup, for whenever some gourmets see sweet corn, they think they can see covered wagons rolling on to California through Sioux Indian territory. And now I must look at my boy's table," he interrupted his strange patter, which I greeted with a foolish giggle, as I pretended to play along with him. "Let's change places," he said, collecting up the dishes after we'd finished the terrific soup, "'canary glitter after graceless prawns: then the second course made its entry as a well-beaten seafood soufflé, bedecked by a quadrille of prawns, a double chorus line of pincers wafting around the steam rising from pastry packed like white coral. The soufflé also contained the celebrated swordfish and lobsters gawking in livid panic as if their carapaces were greeting the torch that burnt out their bulging eyes.'" I couldn't find words to praise the soufflé, and this shortfall of mine or of my language, turned out to be the best praise of all. "'After a dish that so successfully preened its strident colors, a flaming Gothic of almost Baroque proportion yet retaining the Gothic in the texture of the dough and the allegories sketched by the prawns, let some light relief into the lunch with this beetroot salad, mayonnaise dressing, Lübeck asparagus'; and keep with us, Juan Carlos Rondon, because we're reaching the climax to the ceremony." And when he went to skewer some beetroot, the whole slice came away and fell on the tablecloth. He couldn't hide his annoyance, and tried to right his error of judgment, but the beet bled again, and at the third attempt the beet fell to pieces where he'd skewered it: one half was left on the fork, and the other slid back on the tablecloth, making three purple islands around the rosettes. I was about to express my dismay, when he gave me an entranced look: "Such perfection," he said, "those three stains make a really splendid setting for our meal." He continued, almost declamatory: "In that light, with the stubborn patience of an artisan, the threads ominously channel the vegetable blood, and the three stains arouse dark expectations." He smiled, delighted in revealing his secret to me: "You are present at the family lunch that doña Augusta regales in the pages of *Paradiso*, chapter seven. Now you can say you've eaten like a real Cuban, and joined once and for all the brotherhood of the Master's admirers, though you're still unfamiliar with his work." Next we ate roast turkey, followed by an equally Lezaman ice cream, the recipe for which he offered me to pass on to my mother. "Bladovino should now bring on the fruit bowl, but I'll go in her absence. I must apologize for the pears and apples which I've put in place of mangos and guavas, they don't go too badly with the mandarins and grapes. Afterward, naturally, we'll take coffee on the balcony while I recite you poems by the much-maligned Zenea, and we'll give the Havana cigars a miss since neither of us likes them. But first," he added with a sudden wave of inspiration as his eyes lighted on the Spanish shawl, "a little flamenco," and he regaled me with a dashing *zapateado*, which he ended abruptly. "It's loathsome," he said flinging the shawl away. "Perhaps one day you'll forgive me, David." Just what I was thinking, for suddenly I started to feel uneasy, because though enjoying the lunch, I couldn't help some nerve ends remaining raw in that feast, on red alert, spectating, concluding that the lobsters, prawns, Lübeck asparagus, and grapes must have been bought in the special shops for diplomats and consequently were proof of his relationship with foreigners, which, in my role as special agent, I should communicate to the comrade who was yet to become my Ismael.

Time went pleasantly by, then one Saturday when I came to tea, Diego only half opened the door. "You can't come in. I've got somebody with me who doesn't want his face to be seen, and I'm having the time of my life. Please come back later." I went off, but only to the other side of the street, in order to see the face of the man who didn't want to be seen. Diego came down straightaway by himself. I saw how nervously he looked up and down the street before turning the corner at top speed. I hurried and caught sight of him getting into a diplomatic car half-hidden down an alleyway. I had to crouch behind a pillar because they shot out. Diego in a diplomatic car! A pain seared through my chest. For Christ's sake, it was all true. Bruno was right, and Ismael was wrong when he said you had to consider these cases individually. No. One must always be on the alert: queers are treacherous by nature, it's all down to original sin. As for me, no way would I be two-faced. I could quite cheerfully forget the whole episode: my reaction had been pure class-instinct. But I couldn't cheer up. It was painful. It really hurts when a friend betrays you, hell, it's really painful, not to say very annoying to discover you've been stupid yet again, that someone else has duped you quite so easily. You feel really sick when you have no choice but to admit the hardliners are right and that you're just another sentimental shit-bag taken for a ride by the first comer. I went to the Malecón, and as usual, nature took on the color of my soul: in a moment the sky became overcast, the noise of thunder got nearer and nearer, and there was a hint of rain in the air. My steps took me straight to the university, in search of Ismael, but I was clear-sighted enough—or whatever, because clear-sightedness doesn't come easily—to realize that I wouldn't survive a third encounter with his clear, penetrating gaze, and I halted in my tracks. The second had come after the Lezaman lunch, when I needed to put my mind to rest before it exploded. "I was mistaken," I told him then, "this fellow's fine, just a poor wretch not worth keeping an eye on." "But didn't you say he was a counterrevolutionary?" was his ironic rejoinder. "Even here we have to recognize that his experience of the Revolution has not been the same as ours. It's difficult to be on the side of someone who's asking you to stop being yourself before he even lets you in. I mean . . ." But I added nothing. I still didn't trust Ismael enough to say what I was thinking. "He's true to himself, acts according to his own lights. He operates with an inner freedom I wish I had as a militant." Ismael smiled at me. What distinguished Diego and Ismael's clear, penetrating gazes (to bring your bit to an end, Ismael, because this isn't your story) is the fact that Diego's gaze only points things out to you, and Ismael's demands you start changing them right away if they're not to his liking. This is why Ismael was the best of the bunch. He would talk about anything under the sun, and when we said goodbye, he would put his hand on my shoulder and say we shouldn't lose sight of one another. I understood he was freeing me from my duties as a special agent and that our friendship was just beginning. What would he think now when I told him what I'd seen? I returned to Diego's block prepared to wait for as long as was necessary. He came back by taxi in the middle of a downpour. I followed him in before he could close the door. "So my boyfriend's gone," he joked. "Why are you looking like that? Don't tell me you're jealous?" "I saw you getting in the diplomatic car." He wasn't expecting that. The color drained from his cheeks, he slumped into a chair, bowed his head. After a moment he looked up; he'd aged ten years. "Come on, I'm waiting." Now we'd have his confessions, regrets, pleas for forgiveness, the name of the counterrevolutionary sect he belonged to and I'd go straight to the police,

I'd go to the police. "I was going to tell you, David, but I did-
n't want you to find out so soon. I'm leaving."

The tone with which Diego had said "I'm leaving" has
terrible connotations for us. It means you're departing the
country forever, that you're erasing yourself from its memory, and it from yours, and, whether you like it or not, you're
agreeing to be labeled a traitor. You agree to that from the
start because it comes with the price of the ticket. Once it's
in your grasp you won't convince anyone you weren't
delighted with your purchase. It's not you, Diego. What
would you do far from Havana, from those dirty, warm
streets and bustling *habaneros*? What would you do in
another city, dear Diego, where Lezama wasn't born and
Alicia Alonso doesn't put in a final appearance every week-
end? A city without bureaucrats and hardliners to criticize,
without a David who is getting to like you? "It's not because
of what you think," he said. "You know I couldn't care less
about the political swings and roundabouts. It's because of
Germán's exhibition. You're not very perceptive, you don't
know the impact it had. They didn't kick him out of his job,
I was the one they kicked out. Germán reached a compro-
mise with them, he's rented a room and is coming to Havana
to work in arts and crafts. I recognize I went too far in
defending his work, that I was undisciplined and acted like
a free agent, took advantage of my position, but so what?
Now I've got that on my record, I'll only get work in the
fields or on building sites, and you tell me what I'd do with
a brick in my hand, where would I put it? It's only a caution,
but who will ever give a job to someone with my looks. I
know it's not fair, that the law's on my side and in the end
they'd have to admit as much and give me compensation.

But what am I going to do? Fight? No way. I'm weak, and there's no place for the weak in your world. On the contrary, you behave as if we didn't exist, as if we were only here to mortify you and reach agreements with the bums in exile. You lead an easy life: you don't suffer an Oedipus complex, you're not tortured by beauty, you didn't have a favorite cat which your father chopped up in front of you so as to make a man of you. It's not impossible to be queer and strong. There are plenty of examples. I know that. But I'm not one of them. I'm weak, I'm terrified about growing old, I can't wait ten or fifteen years for you to have second thoughts, however confident I am the Revolution will finally change its ways. I'm thirty. At most I've got twenty years of active life left. I want to do things, live, make plans, see myself in the mirror of *Las meninas,* give a lecture on the poetry of Flor and Dulce María Loynaz. Don't I have that right? If I were a good Catholic and believed in another life I wouldn't worry, but your materialism is contagious, that's too many years to wait. This is our life, there is no other. Or at any rate, there's probably only this one. Do you understand? They don't want me here, why mess around, I like the way I am, I want to drop a few pansy petals now and then. Who could that possibly upset, honey, if they're my petals?"

His final days here weren't all sad. Sometimes I found him euphoric, flapping around among parcels and old papers. We drank rum and listened to music. "Before they come to make an inventory, take this typewriter, the electric stove and can opener. Your mom will find it useful. These are my studies on architecture and town planning: a lot of them, right? Very good, too. If I don't have time, send them anonymously to the City Museum. These are the eyewitness accounts of Federico García Lorca's visit to Cuba. It includes a very detailed itinerary and photographs of places and people with captions written by me. Here's an unidentified black. Keep for yourself the poetry anthology to the river Almendares, add whatever poem you feel like, though the Almendares is in no state for poetry. Look at this photo: me in the Literacy Campaign. And these are family photos. I'll take them all with me. This uncle of mine was really gorgeous, he choked on a stuffed potato. This is me with Mom, what a good-looking woman. Let's see, what else do I want to leave you? You've already taken my papers, haven't you? Send whatever articles you think more digestible to *Revolución y Cultura*, where perhaps someone may appreciate them; choose nineteenth-century topics, they get through more easily. Hand over the rest to the National Library, you know to whom. Don't lose that contact, take him the occasional cigar and don't get upset if he makes a pass at you, that's as far as it will go. I'll also give you my contact at the ballet. As for these cups, David Alvarez, the ones we've drunk so much tea from, I want to lend them to you. If you ever get the opportunity, send them to me. As I said, they're Sèvres porcelain. But that's not why, they belonged to the Loynaz del Castillo family, and are a present. Okay, I'll be frank, I filched them. My records and books have already gone, you've taken what were yours and the ones left are to kid the inventory takers. Get me a poster of Fidel with Camilo, a small Cuban flag, the photo of Martí in Jamaica and Mella wearing a hat; but be quick, they've got to go by diplomatic bag with the photos of Alicia in *Giselle* and my collection of Cuban coins and bank notes. Do you want the umbrella or the shawl for your mom?" I kept putting everything away quietly, then I'd get hopeful and hand them back: "Diego, why don't we write to someone. Think of who we could try. Or let me go and ask for an appointment with a government official, and you wait outside." He looked at me sadly and would have none of it. "Do you know any lawyer, any of that suspect lot who is still around? Or somebody in a high-up position who's a closet queer? You've helped lots of people. I graduate in July, in October I'll be working, I can give you fifty pesos a month." I shut up when I saw his eyes watering, though he always managed to recover. "My final piece of advice: choose the clothes you wear carefully. You're no Alain Delon, but you have charm and that air of mystery which can open doors, whatever people say." I was at a loss for words, looked down and started to reorganize and tie up his parcels. "No! Don't unwrap that. They're Lezama's unpublished papers. Don't look at me like that. I swear I'll never misuse them. I also swore to you I'd never go and I am leaving, but this is different. I'll never bargain with them or hand them over to anyone who can manipulate them politically. I swear. By my mother, the basketball player, and you as well, so there. If I can brave the storm without using them, I'll send them back to you. Don't look at me like that! Do you think I don't understand my responsibilities? But if I'm in a tight spot, they might get me out of it. You've made me feel guilty. Pour me a drink and go."

As the date of his departure approached, he languished. He slept badly and lost weight. I spent as much time with him as I could, but he didn't say very much. I think sometimes he couldn't even see me. Curled up in John Donne's armchair with a book of poems and a crucifix, his religiosity had now intensified, he seemed pallid and lifeless. A soft, soothing María Callas lulled him. One day he stared at me really intensely (you're still here, Diego, I'll not forget that look of yours) "Tell me the truth, David," he asked, "do you love me? Has my friendship been of any use? Was I ever disrespectful? Do you think I'm damaging the Revolution?" María Callas stopped singing. "Ours has been a correct friendship and I'm grateful to you." He smiled. "You don't change, do you. I'm not talking about being grateful but of love between friends. Please, don't let's be afraid of words anymore." That was also what I meant, right? But it's difficult for me, and yes he could be sure of my affection and that, to a certain extent, I was someone else, that I'd changed in the course of our friendship, I was more the person I'd always wanted to be. I added: "I invite you to lunch tomorrow at the Bunny Rabbit. I'll go early and get in line. You only have to get there just before twelve. I'll pay. Or would you rather I came for you and we went together?" "No, David, that's not necessary. Everything's okay the way it's been." "Yes, Diego, I insist. I know what I'm saying." "All right, but not the Bunny Rabbit. I'm going vegetarian in Europe." But if what I wanted, or needed, was to put myself on show with him, if that helped to give me peace of mind or something, all right, he would accept. He came to the restaurant at ten to twelve, as people were crowding around the doorway, under a Japanese parasol, in a rig-out that enabled me to spot him two blocks away. He shouted both my surnames across the street, waving an arm weighed down with bracelets. When he was next to me, he kissed me on the cheek and started describing a divine dress he'd just seen in a shop window, which would suite me to a T; to his and my surprise, and those in line, I defended another style so emphatically it quite eclipsed him, because we shy types do shine when we put ourselves out. Our lunch was a celebration of the efficiency of his technique for unbuttoning Communists. And turning to my literary sensibility, he added other titles to my reading list. "Don't forget Countess Merlin, start researching her. You and that woman will have an encounter which will be the talk of the town." We finished up with dessert in Coppelia, and then to his Den for a bottle of Stolichnaya. He was great company until the drink ran out. "I needed this Russian vodka to say two last things to you. David, I think you're rather lacking in initiative. You should be more determined. Your role should be that of an actor, not a spectator. I can assure you this time you'll play it better than in *A Doll's House*. Don't stop being a revolutionary. You'll ask who am I to tell you that. But I do have my moral code, I told you once I'm a patriot and a Lezama Liman. The Revolution needs people like you, because what the Yankees won't manage, the food, the bureaucracy, their kind of propaganda and arrogance, will put an end to, and only people like you can help prevent that. It won't be easy, I can tell you, you'll need lots of courage. The other thing I have to tell you, let's see if I can, because it's really embarrassing, give me the last drop of vodka, that's right: do you remember when we met in Coppelia? That day I gave you a bad time. None of it was chance. I was with Germán, and when we saw you, we laid a bet that I'd bring you to my Den and bed you. It was a bet in foreign currency, I accepted it to get my courage up to take you on, since you had always inspired a respect I found paralyzing. When I spilt the milk over you, it was part of the plan. Your shirt next to the Spanish shawl, draped over the balcony, were the symbols of my victory. Naturally, Germán has spread it around, and more so now he hates me. In some circles, because of late I've been seen only with you, they call me the Red Queen, and others think that my departure is only a pretext, that really I'm a spy with a mission in the West. Don't get too upset, for if such doubts exist about a man, they're not damaging, they make him mysterious and lots of women fall into his arms attracted by the idea of bringing him back to the right path. Will you forgive me?" I said nothing, which he interpreted positively, that I did forgive him. "You see, I'm not the angel you thought I was. Could you have done such a thing behind my back?" We looked at each other. "All right, I will make a last cup of tea. Then you must go and not come back. I don't want any goodbyes." And that was that. When I got out in the street, a line of Pioneers blocked my way. They were wearing freshly ironed uniforms and carrying bunches of flowers; and although a Pioneer with a bunch of flowers had for ages been a tired emblem of the future, inseparable from slogans exhorting us to struggle for a better world, I liked them, perhaps because of that, and I stared at one of them, who stuck his tongue out when he noticed me; and then I told him (I told, didn't promise) that I would defend the next Diego to cross my path tooth and nail, though nobody would understand me, and that wouldn't distance me from my Spirit and Conscience; quite the contrary, if you thought about it, it would be fighting for a better world for you, Pioneer, and for myself. And I wanted to bring the chapter to a close by finding a way to thank Diego for all he had done for me, and I did so by coming to Coppelia and asking for this particular ice cream. Because there was chocolate on the menu but I'd ordered strawberry.

Translated by Peter Bush

Paradiso

José Lezama Lima

WHEN DEMETRIO was on the Isle of Pines he didn't know how to establish himself with the women of the middle class who sat on their front porches after five in the afternoon, or among the other women who sat, also after five in the afternoon, excessively painted, in the houses with parrot-green blinds at the edge of town, nibbling stale bread and sipping sour milk. With the island girls, modest maidens in the shadow of their guardian mothers, he felt timid, incomplete. He thought they looked down on him merely because he had come to the Isle of Pines to find work. His frustration there resounded like a brass horn blown by a circus clown. It was also his opinion that the parents of those maidens would feel more comfortable with a rustic they knew who had a little position, a professional man with relatives in the region, rather than somebody from Havana who, by the very fact that he had had to leave the capital, bore the imprint of all his previous failures. Moreover, he was chubby, bald, short, a poor conversationalist: all that served to keep him in ambush when he met an eligible woman. In the presence of the other women, the ones on the outskirts, covered with creams and cheap perfume, mouths overflowing with lipstick, at an age when the scant voluptuousness of their scaly lips gave them the look of evil beasts of heraldry, he gladly freed himself of his feeling of inferiority, overthrowing its censorship, and loaded himself up with quarrelsome wine, making outbursts and lurching gestures to release his animality with the disjointed passion of primitive people.

In moments of leisure he would take refuge in the pool parlor at the edge of town. It had a woman attendant, neither taken by the pleasure that is given or sold, nor elevated to the prissiness of excessive rejection. She was part Indian, plump, talkative, aggressive, extremely superstitious. She lived comfortably inside her oracular dreams, and in remembering those spells she could determine whether the black cat in the world of sleep ran from right to left, from one rank of the armies to another. She was an ordinary gambling attendant, holding bets, racking balls. Her breadth, revealing a not too distant Tlaxcaltecan forebear, would advance between belligerent parties whenever the usual poolhall arguments grew heated. She had a reputation for dispensing justice without appeal between opponent gamblers. She carried a cue with the serene elegance with which the goddess of intelligence holds her lance. When the combatants hurled themselves into the whirlwind of the fight, the attendant, Blanquita by name, would give her cue a good spin and lay into the visible ribs of the feisty customers, who letting out a shout would disappear in a cloud of dust with bluebottle flies.

Over the islanders Blanquita exercised a universal monarchy of kindness. She dispensed aspirin, appeared at wakes the second night, reconciled couples for the enfilade in the total Hymenaeus. Plump, woebegone, and kind, what worried her least was to approach men out of motives of sexual inferiority. She was an archetypical mother to the whole town, with a pineal eye for suspecting crisis in someone else's emptiness, in his disguised desperation. She would appear with a voice, a skin, a confidence that was something like a custard apple changed into a flowing unguent. With honeyed shadow she would approach the person who, as she drew closer, would drift into sleepy surrender. Her radius, not her female condition, was fruit-bearing, as was her sloth, and whoever approached her felt like a sea slug bounding off a mossy reef, amid soft advice and cottoned carnality.

One day the attendant left her poolhall and hid for a few weeks in the town hotel. Dr. Santurce had decided to weigh anchor in view of the islanders' exceeding slowness to visit his office. It cost him more to keep his whites *scientific*, we might say, on the hotel's wicker chairs, than to pay his collector at the end of the month with the receipts he had saved. For his part, Demetrio had assayed the quality of the calcium in the island water, which kept the ivory of their teeth unbending. The farmers, as if under oath, preferred to let their teeth turn to carbon rather than see them at the end of Dr. Demetrio's pincers. The more he assured them of painless extractions, the more his potential patients seemed fixated in a crisis of masochism, holding themselves upright in the darkness where the growth of caries was a slash in the living red.

The years that followed the death of doña Cambita, Demetrio's mother, the hearer's daughter, had softened him with their sad solitude. Blanquita, with her unguents, had been transformed into a Marian intercessor between his frustration and his fate. One day, when Demetrio was complaining about his failure on the Isle of Pines, Blanquita counseled him, as happens in certain Oriental legends, that perhaps he had come there only to be able to return to Havana one day, and then his cup of plenty would smile and overflow. "I can see you now," she told him, "living in a big house in the Cerro district, with the large living room divided into two parts, one for your office and the other for the waiting room, and I'll see to it," she said in all innocence, "that the newspapers are fresh, so the patients won't get bored, or at least not quite so bored, since the news is generally boring anyway. In the center of the courtyard there'll be a high-spouting fountain. And we'll have a big cage with a monkey full of tricks and mischief. And a blue jay in a little cage. In the anteroom, a table with drawers full of payments. I'll keep the key, not because I'm interested in money, but so you won't squander it."

One day Uncle Alberto took José Cemí by the arm and brought him to Demetrio's house in El Cerro. It was dazzling, with the monkey by the fountain in the center of the courtyard. The sun shone on the copper wires of the cage, and the blue jay came forward to gild his breast. Another big cage, filled with birds the size of a forefinger, burst into motion as if a head of hair were swimming in a rainbow tremor. Three or four Sundays passed, and again he was taken to Demetrio's house. Cemí froze, perplexed. The monkey near the fountain was no longer enraptured, his face of unifying, meditative concentration, his noises of a toad's guitar. The fountain, coldly, did not mourn his absence. The blue jay, once gigantized by man, had found the strength and subtlety to push open the small door of his jail and had drowned his own blue in that of the sky above. All the little sparks in the large cage had hidden themselves, restless spirits that had finally found their repose. The change in setting brought the fascination of two atmospheres to Cemí. He recalled the morning gold of his first visit, braided out as in certain Venetian painters who weave snakes of polished copper into resting hair.

The day he discovered the absence of the pleasant colored motifs of the house was a humid Sunday, almost misty, putting great wet cloths over objects and faces, wet cloths like the ones sculptors use to cover plaster figures to bridge the space between repose and reencounter in the course of extracting their form. Cemí perceived that the fascination of the big house did not depend on any particular presence or contingency, such as the enclosure or absence of the blue jay, the monkey's skill in rescuing a nut from the top of the fountain. On the contrary, it seemed an abandonment to dreams, births, Christmas greetings, or visions of agony. The great central courtyard, the emptiness around it, the living room, the bedrooms, and at the end of the courtyard the noble kitchen, with its barrel of charcoal, with its night that suddenly passes into a carbuncle and begins to give off planetoids.

Demetrio chatted interminably with doña Augusta about the benefits of his new status, about his new house after his marriage to Blanquita, the poolroom attendant. Her care for the blue jay, for the receipts from extractions and fillings. Demetrio tried to make his conversation pleasant, easygoing; being perfectly aware of the blood in his family, he sensed some unpleasantry between Augusta and her irregular son. He was well acquainted with Alberto's weakness for spirits and the manner in which the fourth drink, according to the Greeks the one of dementia, led to street-corner improvisations of the babbling prophecies of minstrelsy. Demetrio was trying to create an atmosphere woven out of peaceful garlands until Leticia and Dr. Santurce arrived, and to transform the scorpion into a male dove that would eat grain from the hand of a Venetian. His familiar, soporific verbosity had almost achieved those effects when, rapid and slim, passing the grating between the main door and the dining-room door, Uncle Alberto was seen, dressed in blue, his face pink from a recent bath, all his pleasant Cuban resourcefulness at work and apparent in his eyes and magically delicate smile. All the lordliness of the Cuban bourgeoisie showed in him, the disdain, the domination of their surroundings, in which they came and went at will, accompanied by certain propitious deities that seemed to wave their hands, calling to approach without fear. It pleased his deities to have given him those gifts and a gracious, pleasant manner, which usually responded by shooting a precise arrow at the hare of the instant.

Alberto Olaya's reaction to the magnet of family demonism was especially Cuban. He would be freely, reverently surrounded. Sometimes the whole family would hang on a single point: trying to guess what would be nice for Alberto. For the family dynasty of the Cemís and the Olayas, the small diabolic dose of Alberto was more than enough. The family watched over and cared for that little devil cat as if he were the end result of a classical and robust development, characterized by smiling good sense and allied to the river of time in which that ark floated with alliances intertwined at the roots. Except for certain small features, Uncle Alberto formed an inaccessible and invisible part of this lustrous family tapestry, as if to receive the caress of the generations.

The adventuresome arrival, along with its feigned demonism, of Blanquita the poolhall attendant, was not contained in the family nucleus, diluted itself in the distance, and furthermore she was the guardian of the house in El Cerro, and when she surrounded herself with her two hundred pounds, she achieved a hieraticism by progressive inactivity, on top of the stone on which his patients would be sacrificed, like those Aztec idols representing the hurricane's powers, inflating their cheeks to eject furious spurts of water, except that in the large house, the hurricane was represented by a molar, which when the flesh was crushed shot a lightning bolt through the whole nervous system. Kindness had created in her an immense adipose tissue that covered everything, there a demonic fiber was a sardine plowing through an oleaginous ocean. A great stone chair, waiting for the devil, would be pressed down by knots of bumps, the ponderous quivering of matter, lard jelled in a refrigerator. Through those many impediments, the devil would be unable to walk and occupy his stone seat.

The mother saw in her son Alberto the incarnation of a whole system of fortifications to defend the thesis of the perfection of certain members of the family, a theory to which most families subscribe as they hand over the gifts and all the other qualitative essences to annul the defects, great and small, in their innocent strayed sheep. These mothers live in ambush for the minor bothers that might afflict this kind of son, to make outsiders believe that all those cares are the result not of exceptional irregularities but of a vast, pious chorus whose goal, in a mysterious paradox, is to press for the inscrutable outcome of a chain of events, which will shatter the style and quality that a family has almost managed to achieve in the course of centuries. The first combat takes place between the mother and the demons who assault the family castle at its weakest tower. This son represents the ultimate sacrifice of reason, and the ultimate mystery. Thus, in the end, a mother may have wanted, in spite of her snood of irrepressible kindness, to be judged demonic too. The same thing as sometimes happens in Greek choruses can happen among members of a family whose bonds of the spirit seem to conquer those of the blood, or among friends who would delight in the same eros: with someone's attributing a greater defect to himself, the choral antistrophe, the relative who loves us or the passionate friend, responds, attributing to themselves invented defects that tend to mitigate the effect produced by the confession of one of the subjects of the unknown laws of human gravity; that is, by virtue of what fatality does that *sympathos* act on those beings, extracting from immense choral masses whole cities nourished by constellations of termites that still imagine they are free, two beings who with the passage of time began to look at each other and who with the passage of time cannot say goodbye without alluding to the precise place in which they will meet again. This may bring one of them to reveal, on a tedious night of rain and shots of whiskey, that as a child he had hidden from his grandmother a basket of flowers that one of her daughters had sent her from some remote province; the other, in order to soothe his friend's aroused subconscious, confesses that one day, left alone at home, he incomprehensibly used the gardener's shears to bisect the Mechlin lace blouse that his grandfather had given his grandmother on the occasion of an anniversary. And that while the poundcake was being sliced, he could not stop thinking with a certain pleasure about his grandmother's face as she examined her blouse and came to the realization that a brutal hand, and one that lived in the same house with her, was capable of penetrating her past with the premeditated malice of a murderer. But most significant was the fact that both stories came forth from the realm of lies. Affected by melancholy drunkenness, the first friend's story was in reality the last confidence of a too anxious girlfriend in whom the spirits had produced a foggy recollection of a springtime cornucopia that had simply been transformed into a basket of flowers. And the other friend had responded in kind, for what he had done in his tale of feigned guilt was to replace real mice with imaginary shears, and unlike the most irascible spinners, he never gripped the fearful implement of Atropos.

Translated by Gregory Rabassa

In the Cold of the Malecón

Antonio José Ponte

"HE CHOPPED the meat into small pieces. Too small."

"Like his apartment," the mother commented.

"Yes . . . And you want to know what I thought, seeing him cut the meat in the kitchen of the tiny apartment?"

She could imagine.

"I thought how strange that we've had a son."

Because they behaved like those old married couples, very attached to one another, who could never have children and in old age each becomes the child of the other.

"It would've been stranger not to have one."

"He was slicing the green bananas into rounds and then removing the skin from each round. You never did it that way."

"No."

She made a pretense of high spirits.

"But the apartment, describe it. What's it like?"

The father began to place all the rooms of the apartment within the room where they were sitting.

"It could all fit in here," he said finally.

So then he hasn't managed to get away from us, the mother thought.

"And tell me if he ate the meat."

The meat was a present they'd sent him.

"He cooked some of the small pieces and we ate them, and during the meal he talked about his work."

"He told you he'll have to move farther away, right?"

"How'd you guess?"

"It's a pretext of his."

"Could be, yes."

"He needs pretexts to defend himself from us," the mother said aloud.

"Did you see things that weren't his? I mean: does he live alone?"

"There was nobody else with us, no. There was one thing that seemed odd to me."

"What?"

"He didn't want the meat to lose the blood in cooking. He ate it very rare."

"And you?"

"Me? The same as always."

The mother nodded

"While you were eating you asked him to take you to see the whores."

"After we had just finished eating. The pieces of meat were hard to stick a fork into. He asked me what I felt like doing. We had three hours before my train left and could take advantage of the time."

"Go on. Go on."

"Near his apartment are some movie theaters. Or we could walk around a little . . . Then I told him I'd like to see the whores again."

"See them again?" The mother burst out laughing. "They can't be the same ones, they'd be wrecks by now."

The father laughed too.

"Of course."

"He knows where to find them," the mother mused aloud.

"He said we could go but that it was a bad night to walk along the Malecón. We might not find any."

"Why a bad night?"

"The surf. The waves crash over the top of the wall of the Malecón. You can't stay there without getting splashed."

"But finally you did find some."

"After a lot of walking. They were on the edge of the sidewalk, being careful of the waves and looking at the cars passing by."

"And they didn't look at you?"

The father suddenly felt ridiculous.

"At me? I'm old."

"At him."

"One woman looked at him for a moment. Just a moment, that's all. Like when you mistake someone in the street and realize the mistake immediately."

"And then?"

"She went back to looking at the street so she wouldn't miss any cars."

"Keep going."

"And that was all. We went back to his apartment to have coffee. I really liked the coffee, it gave me a lift. I asked him if he'd seen how that woman had looked at him."

"Yes."

"And in spite of how strange it was being his father, it felt right, the two of us in the nice warmth of his apartment, the two of us there and those women outside in the cold of the Malecón."

There the story ended. The two old people were silent for a while.

"Tell me again," the mother asked.

"What do you want me to tell you?"

"The way she looked at him, the woman you found."

Translated by Cola Franzen

Life on the Rooftops

Pedro Juan Gutiérrez

I WAS LIVING a little more comfortably. I managed to get a room on a roof with just two neighbors. And I had to give up the beer-can business. There was lots of competition, and we were forced to scuffle like dogs in the dumpsters of Miramar. Sometimes I couldn't even come up with twenty empty cans in a morning. Now I had a new business, and I was doing better for myself.

The room was clean, with a kerosene stove, its own bathroom, and lots of fresh air. It was on the ninth floor of another building near the Malecón, with a view of the sea. The neighbors weren't bad: an old married couple, always screaming and fighting, and a bolero singer and his wife.

I had known the singer fifteen years ago. In those days, he had his own group and he was young. Armandito Villalón and the Comets. They played catchy little songs. Some were picked as "the neighborhood hit of the week" at the radio station where I worked. Then Armandito got desperate for money. He disbanded the group and started singing solo with cassette backup in three clubs every night. He made a lot of money singing the same boleros over and over, until his voice was ruined and his stomach ulcer turned into cancer from all his rum and cigarettes. He had a heart attack and he was skinny, starving, and wrinkled. The country was seized by the crisis of the nineties, and on top of everything else, he went looking for more trouble: he joined a group for the defense of human rights. He was up against the wall. Every so often, on the slightest of pretexts, he was locked up in jail for a few days, side by side with real criminals.

It was around that time we started to see each other again. I was his new neighbor, and I said hello to him the way I used to, when I was working at the radio station and he was recording his little songs. But the man was bitter, irritable, obsessed with freedom and human rights. And hungry. He only had one gig, at the Salem Club, Fridays to Sundays. The Salem is a hellhole in downtown Havana. One night I went to have a few drinks and, while I was at it, listen to some of Armandito's boleros. I couldn't get in because the door was barred and there was a fat black man, as fierce as a gorilla, who was in charge of locking and unlocking it. I didn't like that scene. I can't be locked up like a prisoner in a disgusting club where they sell bad rum for a hundred bucks a glass. The man told me that's how they keep fights under control until the police arrive. "If there's a brawl, I lock the door and no one comes out until I let them out, ha, ha, ha," said the idiot, who had the face of a mental retard.

I mentioned it to Armandito the next day, and it became the theme of another speech on human rights: "Yes, we've lost all self-respect. This country is a prison, a repressive system lodged inside each person's head. The solution to any problem is to impose rules, bars, barriers, discipline, control. It's unbearable, Pedro Juan."

I just said, "You're going to drive yourself crazy, pal. I can barely deal with my own problems, so tell me why I should get myself mixed up with politicians, who are sons of bitches and in the end just do whatever their dicks tell them to do. It's the same no matter where you are. Politics is the art of the scam."

And he replied angrily, "That's exactly why we are the way we are. Because of pessimism and conformism. We've got to confront all of that and denounce it. We've got to fight and speak the truth." The man was a live wire. He always talked about the same thing. If he didn't stop, he'd be in electroshock treatment soon.

On the roof he kept a chicken coop and two pigs. They were obsessed with those animals, he and his wife. They spent hours sitting by the cage, staring at them, mesmerized, feeding them vegetable peelings. Ever since the crisis began, in 1990, lots of people had been raising chickens and pigs on their patios, on roofs, in the bathroom. That way they had something to eat. The wife worked in a worker's cafeteria and she brought home scraps for the animals. She was skinny and ravaged too. Around the same time he had cancer and his heart attack, Armandito got a divorce. He left his apartment to his first wife and their two children, and he came to live in the room on the roof with the mulatta. At the time, she was lovely, a tall, beautiful woman with the happy, mischievous grace of mulattas. Not anymore. Now she was withered, too skinny, though sometimes she still flashed sparks.

The old couple in the other room had a pigeon house, too, and a chicken coop. They sold the pigeons for *santería*. The old man was a *santero*. And he never talked. He was the sullen type. Always squabbling with the old lady. I never found out anything about them. They barely said hello. That's how it is. They hate you because you're white. So, fine. I never got to know them, nor did I care to.

I had no problems when it was cold and there was a strong wind off the sea. But in April, when it started to be hot and it was dead calm, there was a stench of shit, and the gnats and mosquitoes moved in. It was unbearable. Neither the old couple nor Armandito washed out their coops. Well, all right. Sometimes they sprinkled a little bit of water around. We had water problems, and we had to carry buckets from the cistern in the basement of the building. Nine floors, no elevator. Every five or six days the water level rose a little higher in the cistern and then it was pumped out of the tank and we could get it from a faucet.

The roof turned into a stinking place, with gnats biting by day and mosquitoes by night. It was impossible to sleep.

In general, I'm not a lover of good smells. Right now I can't even remember any particular woman's perfume. I don't like smells like that. Either that, or they don't interest me. On the other hand, I'll never forget the smell of the fresh shit of a boy attacked by sharks in the Gulf of Mexico. He was a tuna fisherman. He was going about his business in the stern of the boat, pulling up the splendid silver fish one by one, when he fell overboard. Three enormous sharks were swimming with the tunas, and in two bites they shredded his guts and ripped off his leg. We hauled him up very quickly, still living, his eyes wide with horror; everything happened in less than a minute. And he died immediately, bled to death, without ever being able to speak or understand what had happened to him. For months we were together in that stern, but I can't remember his face or his name. All I can remember clearly is the terrible stink of the boy, with his abdomen slashed open and his guts spilling excrement onto the boat's deck.

There have been other terrible smells in my life, but I don't want to talk about them anymore. Enough of that.

The smell of the chicken and pig shit started to attract more cockroaches. There had always been cockroaches, but now there were more. And rats: huge animals that came up from the basement of the building, almost eighty feet below. They came up the drainpipes, ran to the cages to eat peelings and scraps, and then plunged down again to their dens.

We plugged up the drainpipes with stones. One day a rat jumped from the toilet bowl and ran through the room to the roof, faster than lightning. I couldn't believe it. It seemed impossible to me that the animal could climb up the sewer pipe and break the water seal of the toilet.

I was pissed. This was too much. I went to talk to Armandito and the old couple, which got me nowhere. They wouldn't move the animals off the roof, even if the rats took over everything and drove us out with their fangs snapping at our heels. On my piece of roof I could do whatever I wanted, but I had no right to ask them to do anything. And they showed me a newspaper clipping about roof laws. I tried not to raise my voice. But I couldn't help it. In the end, I told them they could all go to hell.

It was August, and it was too hot. I was fed up with arguing, and I thought about poisoning all the animals. I found my two strychnine seeds in a tight twist of paper. I had picked them up in the botanical garden at Cienfuegos, at the foot of a strychnine tree. Some latent criminal instinct made me keep them for so many years. I thought about how I might sneak up to the cages at night and give the animals the poison mixed with a little rice. But I would be found out. It was better to wait and kill them little by little. And what if the old people ate the dead animals and they died too? Shit, what do you know, a little detective novel was already taking shape. The heat, the humidity, the gnats biting, the stink of shit. And me with no idea how the hell to poison those animals. I needed a little fresh air. I took the four dollars I had left, and I went to San Rafael Boulevard to try to sell them. Hopefully a peasant would come along and I could hit him up for sixty. The exchange had dropped from 120 pesos to 50 in a little less than a month. The government wanted to manage the crisis by sweeping up everything: pesos and dollars. It seemed to me that people were poorer and hungrier than ever, but at least all of the money was safe in the king's coffers.

As I was walking along Galiano toward San Rafael, a light-skinned mulatto shot past me like an arrow, and behind him came a peasant with a knife in his hand, shouting, "Cut him off, cut him off!" I didn't cut anybody off. The peasant ran past me. It seemed he had been sold some counterfeit bills, and by the time he realized it the man was already far away.

Then I was told that the peasant caught up with the man and stabbed him in the shoulder, and a policeman punched him a few times too. It's a good trick, but people already know it and it's hard to get away with it: you paste a number five or twenty, cut from a photocopy of a bill of the appropriate denomination, over the one on each corner of a one-dollar bill. It works if you hand the money over quickly, in a dark place, and you cover up Washington with your thumb. You've got to find a guy who's in a hurry to trade and, above all, travel light and make a quick getaway.

I got to San Rafael and I was there for a few hours, but no buyers showed up. There were lots of people selling . . . And hardly any peasants. They're the ones with money. They make their fortunes out of people's hunger. It's a new era. All of a sudden, money is necessary. As always, money crushes everything in its path. Thirty-five years spent constructing the new man. And now it's all over. Now we've got to make ourselves into something different, and fast. It's no good to fall behind.

Translated by Natasha Wimmer

My Aunt Leocadia,
Love, and the Lower Paleolithic

Calvert Casey

THE OTHER AFTERNOON I went into that enormous storehouse of useful and useless things that in Cuba we call "the Ten-Cen" and that the Americans built with the name "Woolworth" on its façade, a name no one could ever pronounce.

In that great club where we've all killed so many afternoons, young people meet and peek at each other furtively across the counters, and the more daring among them may arrange a romantic rendezvous in a dark movie house or at the little hotel on the Calle Rayo, only to stop loving each other afterward and go back to peeking furtively across the same counter and trying to stay out of each other's aisle; there are well-dressed ladies who down enormous quantities of food in the midst of the tremendous racket while they tell each other about their ailments, their faces glowing with a hard determination to keep on living; and, among many other things, there are faded gentlemen who go there to let their hands stray among the females jammed against the showcases.

As I was mulling over the possibility of a *café con leche* it occurred to me that, alas, young people had the disadvantage of having no memories and not even knowing that not many years ago the Ten-Cen had stood at the corner of Amistad where now there was a shop, with two towers, run by two solidly middle-class Spaniards, and on the opposite corner there'd been a café with enormous mirrors where the fat politicians with their Panama hats would go to spend the afternoon and which had some private rooms facing Rayo that with their conspiratorial air represented for me the height of sinfulness. But then it seemed to me that very old people would probably think that, alas, in comparison with them I had no memories and didn't even know what you could get in the Ten-Cen before there was any building with two towers, and that in turn the dead were probably feeling sorry for them because they had no memories of when there were no sidewalks on that corner and the street wasn't paved and slaves crossed it on their daily errands, or peasants bringing provisions to the city from the nearby farms, and feeling greater pity or even greater envy for those who are yet to be born, who have no memories and who in turn, once they're old or dead, will pity or envy their descendants for the absence or the ever-renewed abundance of memories. And I thought of something I'd never thought of before while a very chubby and very beautiful waitress served me my *café con leche* as I sat by the entrance from San Miguel. I thought that the dead would always outnumber the living, that the sum of those who have died will always be vastly greater than the sum of those who at any given moment live on the earth, and that the number of the dead is swelling constantly; and in my mind I reread the obituaries in the morning paper and I understood that kind of

satisfaction that I always feel when I read them, the satisfaction of a mathematician who sees his calculations confirmed with every passing day. I thought that we live surrounded by the dead, on top of the dead, vast numbers of
the dead who are quietly waiting for us in the cemeteries of
the world, at the bottom of the sea, in the countless layers
of the earth that will never again see the sun; and perhaps,
without our even noticing it, their ashes are in the cement
with which we build our houses, or in the cup we raise to
our lips every morning, ashes of faces and eyes and hands,
which stay with us as long as we live and surround us and
are by our side and beneath us and on top of us. I thought
of the world's huge depositories of bones that turn into dust
that the wind scatters and we breathe in, and I thought of
the fourth of May 1894 and the twenty-eighth of August
1903 and a day in the year 328 B.C. and of all the millions of
human beings who were alive at that moment and making
love and deflowering virgins and sobbing and stabbing a
brother and masturbating and eating and buying honey and
thinking what I'm thinking right now and going to war and
treating their sores, and of whose lives nothing remains,
nothing, nothing at all, not the slightest memory, because
the buildings that housed their lives have already turned to
dust and the papers on which they wrote their names have
disintegrated and their dust lies beneath many layers of
earth that perhaps a bulldozer dug up yesterday morning
and a man turned into cement with which another man
built the wall on which our hands are resting at this very
moment.

The day before, I'd been in the National Library, and
carefully, because they were falling apart in my hands, I'd

started to leaf through the 1910 issues of a magazine that came out on Saturdays and in which an artist illustrated the week's tragedies: "The Crime in El Guatao," "Her Throat Slit by Jealous Husband during Performance at the Payret," "A Brightly Lit Suicide," "Peasants Hanged Nude in La Luisa," "The Knifing of Tulipán," and so on; or the artist went to the morgue and drew profiles of the bodies lying ever so quietly on the zinc-topped autopsy tables with their crushed skull or the trench running across their neck from ear to ear and the sharp borders of the wound that let you see the beginning of the trachea, or with their head completely cut in two, lying there peacefully on the zinc table-top, or with the dark furrow of the hanged and their dry mouth half open and the lids half closed over the eyes or one eyeball burst from its socket, or the head of the old black man who turned up dead on the Cerro and on whom they found a piece of paper that said, "I am 140 years old, I was born in the Congo and sold in Havana in 1787," and who knows who wrote it and stuck it in his pocket so that when he died they'd know he was over a hundred; and so the artist filled up his sheet with the profiles of the dead, and as I thought of them I asked myself whether nothing was left of them, whether no one would ever, ever remember them anymore, and the few who did remember them would soon be dead. And I asked myself whether nothing, nothing at all was left, then, of black Pablo Dupuy and the American they found in the bathtub at the Hotel Plaza and the Irish sailor Farrell whose skull was crushed on the Alameda de Paula and the girl I saw yesterday on the corner of Industria and the delicate blue veins of her breasts and the Chinaman Lon Fuy whom they burned on the

Calle Soledad and white Esperanza Otero who hanged herself and the homeless mulatto who fell asleep at La Ciénaga and the train cut off his head while he was sleeping. Nothing left of our profiles, calm in death, and our dry mouths and our half-closed eyelids and our slit throats, our bodies mutilated or battered by sickness? And will there be no one to speak of us far off in the next millennium, several meters above us, and we several meters above all the unknown millions who preceded us?

I poured some sugar in my cup, and as I slowly stirred it I set to calculating the number of human beings who have died; but when I finished I realized I'd fallen short.

Feeling a little better, I looked around me. The crowd continued to churn, with those streaming in from San Miguel bumping into those coming from inside the great store. The place was brilliantly lit. In the midst of the throng, a man on a ladder was replacing a sign that said "Giant Raspberry Supercake" with one that said "Hot Dogs, 15 centavos."

The air conditioning, set very high, made me shiver a bit. I drank a sip of my *café con leche*, which was still warm, and then added a little more sugar. I looked down at the clean granite floor that a boy swept whenever the crowd thinned out a little. My imagination toyed with the fate of those few square meters of ground where perhaps only a century before, when this had been a poor district on the edge of town, had stood a wooden house with trees and maybe with a cow, and a century farther back an as-yet-undivided estate held under a royal grant, and two centuries farther back a forest of palms and *yagrumas*, and right there beneath the row of identical chairs where the ladies were chewing, maybe there was a path and a man ran down it fleeing from someone or just because he felt like running, and I reconstructed the forest, which had been dislodged to make way for countless forms of life and where only stealthy or peaceful men had walked, and before them, only frightened animals.

Gradually I came to realize that the very space where I was sitting, surrounded and buffeted by the clamoring crowd rushing to buy one last toothbrush before closing time, had been the patio of my aunt's house, where, in violation of every public health ordinance, she had planted a small ceiba tree in a large tub, and it had gotten too big for the tub and grown as high as the rooms of the upstairs apartment in search of sunlight, and she'd planted some basil and several rickety rosebushes; that the space occupied by the sinks and the shiny coffee urns and the advertisements for ice cream and milkshakes, right in front of me, had been her room, the front room of the huge house, the room with the high-legged wardrobe with the mirror, full of turn-of-the-century clothes and very sumptuous yellowed bed linens. A little farther on, where a noisy group of schoolboys on their way home from school was slurping up large dishes of ice cream, my great-grandmother had died, after spending her days in an armchair next to her bed, in the company of her cat, which slept all day on her lap and which disappeared when she died. From time to time one of her granddaughters would come and undertake the delicate operation of bathing the old woman.

For a moment I stopped hearing the constant noise of the Ten-Cen and remembered that the room opened onto the patio, that it smelled of dried flowers and earth and moldy leaves and damp towels and bedpans that needed emptying and floors washed with buckets of water. A door led out to the patio; the other door had a grill that reached up to the ceiling; every now and then a rooster would perch on the tub and crow; and seen from inside the room, through the grill, the patio had the melancholy intimacy of all the patios in Havana. Every room was a world apart, separated from the others by the doors of frosted glass crowned by a lacework of wooden roses; and when the sun reached the tubs in the patio the light streamed into every room and a swarm of insects blinded by the light rose from the rotting earth.

All of that had been reduced to the endless black counter and the chewing schoolboys and the tremendous din of the store and the background music seeping through the hubbub and the chill of the air conditioning.

I knew my Aunt Leocadia in her last years. In what had been the parlor of the old house on the Calle San Miguel, a showcase with cracked glass panes announced to the world that my aunt was a dressmaker skilled in pleating and embroidery. Everybody talked about my aunt's rich customers, but I never saw anyone come through the door that had been a window in the last century and whose grill was rusting away on the patio floor, behind the ceiba. Now and then the room would shake with the vibrations from complicated electric machines. That meant my aunt was making lace.

But my curiosity and the mysteries began in her room, which I could only glimpse when she opened the doors to take some money out of the huge wardrobe that no one but she ever opened. Gradually I came to know the room's secrets. There was a brass bed with a light switch resting on the pillow and connected to an ancient blue lightbulb hanging from the ceiling, and a dressing table with two purple lamps hand-decorated by my aunt and a powder box with gilded feet and two worm-eaten paintings, because my aunt had studied art at the Academy of San Alejandro. When I remembered that one of the paintings showed the pond in the Quinta de los Molinos, with the artificial island in the middle of the greenish water covered with *suche* leaves, I laughed to myself, and the beautiful chubby waitress stopped and gave me a somewhat hostile look. I avoided her eyes and recalled the time my aunt got sick and they let me go in to see her. She was lying on worn and not very clean sheets and scolding somebody for wanting to use the bed linens, embroidered years before, that she kept in the wardrobe and that no one, but no one, was allowed to touch.

I remembered that my aunt had been forced to sublet the back rooms and those of the upper story to tenants who never paid and who engaged in epic battles that frequently brought on the intervention of the police. A wall separated my aunt's rooms from these others; but one could keep track of her neighbors' private lives by the frequency of their fights, during which they shouted at the top of their lungs.

I suspect that my aunt protected herself against that hostile world by shutting her room off from the outside world. On more than one Sunday I found her completely alone in her vast apartment, going over her out-of-fashion dresses and her linen and batiste bedclothes. I supposed that only the chosen of her heart would be admitted into her sexagenarian virgin's room. Later I found out that the frosted glass doors had been opened several times with ever-fresh faith, only to be closed again, leaving the room's inhabitant ever alone.

Over the years I'd always heard the stories they told in the family about my aunt and in fact often asked to hear them. Once, on the beach in Matanzas, shortly after independence, she'd saved a reckless bather from death, swimming an enormous distance with her in tow. When my aunt emerged from the waves pulling the rash but rescued woman by the hair, the crowd applauded, stirred less by the rescuer's deed than by her splendid figure. I laughed again, out loud this time, partially covering my face with my right hand. Two clerks stared at me and whispered to each other.

My aunt's first suitor had died a tragic death. Someone had shot him during the violent early years of the century. She mourned him deeply and never spoke of him again. If the topic came up in her presence she fell silent.

My aunt's next disappointment in love inflicted deeper wounds that clouded her judgment, never very clear, for a whole long and painful year. Contemporary rumor, which was fond of linking pathology and black magic, attributed her derangement to some powders dropped into a cup of coffee. The fact is that as a result of her unfortunate experience my Aunt Leocadia fell into a stupor that lasted exactly a year. The doctors saw no hope for her; and the family had to be constantly on guard to keep my aunt, who refused to put on any clothes except such underwear as was indispensable for covering her nakedness, from going out into the street to the delight and amusement of the irreverent young folk of the Calle San Miguel and the great anxiety of all the neighbors. Her recovery was as strange and unexpected as her illness. The industrious women of the family had undertaken to embroider a gala cape for a traveling bullfighter, but the work could not proceed beyond a certain point. There was a flaw in the design that destroyed the symmetry of the figures. Suddenly my aunt emerged from her stupor, stood up, and, as she pointed out the mistakes made in embroidering, shook off the deranging influence for good, and the matador could continue on his tour. This episode, too, my aunt never again mentioned; and when I asked her something about it one day, I was met with an icy silence.

I don't know how long after that it was (my aunt had become quite prosperous) that a man came to the house whom she introduced as her partner and who proceeded to settle in the patio, far beyond the tub and the iron washstands. I tried to remember whether this guest had come to the house as one more tenant and the partnership had developed later, or whether the agreement had come first and the partner had then settled by the headquarters of the business. My aunt, over forty now, was still beautiful. She no longer went to the Quinta de los Molinos on Sunday afternoons to paint. With the optimism of those boom days of the twenties, she now believed in the virtues of money and, as always, in the possibility of love. She bought stock in banks that would soon fail and take all her savings down with them. I never heard anyone speak well of her guest, whose arrival no one in the family has ever been able to explain and who was much younger than she. I know my aunt adored him. Her collection of embroidered robes and her less yellowed laces stem from this period.

But the man had bad habits, a passion for the fruit of other people's labor, deep admiration for his own good looks, and a somewhat excessive love of the good life. Once I caught my aunt looking at an old portrait. It was of him. When his real aims became clear and the profits from the business began to go astray before reaching their sanctuary in the front room, my aunt let him take his handsome profile and his questionable habits elsewhere. The breakup must have been a painful one. On rare occasions, when everybody had already forgotten about him, she would suddenly mention him, like someone who wants to get over an unpleasant memory by talking about it.

One day somebody solemnly announced to the family, "Aunt Leocadia's touched her trigeminal."

They all started to get their trigeminals touched and of course that eventually produced a sneeze. My aunt did not recover her youth, nor did anyone else; and the Spanish doctor who guaranteed that touching that small nerve at the base of the nose would not only restore youth but cure every ailment ended his visit to Havana a little richer than when he'd come.

At that time a widower used to visit my aunt. I remember that on Sundays she began to take her faded gowns and other garments out of the wardrobe and dress herself up to receive him. My aunt's new suitor was a heavy, boisterous man clad entirely in white and starched even to his tie. He sported ivory-handled canes, a watch chain and fob, showy tie pins, and a heavy gold watch. He lived off the ill-gotten opulence of the most recent conservative cabinet and spoke of it as Milton does of Paradise lost, but unlike Milton he counted on returning to Eden. My aunt listened to him with fascination. The man talked constantly about an invisible princely past, and the family came to be enraptured with his collection of canes.

At that point I realized I ought to leave. I felt the curiosity of my neighbors at the counter as they kept close watch on me; but I couldn't do anything but stir what was left of my coffee with a stubborn movement of my hand and the spoon, my eyes glued to my empty glass, while the noise continued to swell.

After a while family rumor had it that the widower had moved in with my aunt. I could see him clearly. He was coarse and common; time and events only accentuated these qualities. He slept surrounded by photos of his dear departed. What my aunt came to know were the dregs of a happy but ever more remote past. The years rolled on and his friends did not return to power; and so the thick watch and its chain soon disappeared, to be rescued from the pawnshop by my aunt every year for the widower's saint's day, and the tie pins and the famous cane collection disappeared, along with the remaining suits stiff with starch, and in their place appeared his children, abandoned for years in public institutions of charity. Gradually they followed their father and moved in, claiming to have jobs that never quite materialized; and my aunt saw her family increased by three huge awkward teenagers somehow bestial in their appearance and habits who wolfed down everything, and by their sister, a lively but clumsy creature who talked constantly and at the top of her lungs about the convent home for indigent girls that she had just left, dwelling morbidly on all the attempted rapes and abductions that had occurred in that holy place, and who reacted violently to any suggestion that she be still.

The family, happy to be reunited, aired its differences by brutally screaming at each other in battles that drove my terrified aunt to seek refuge in her room.

These new inhabitants of the house, along with the depressed economy, drove away my aunt's family and her clientele; and she was left alone, with only the widower to defend her from the attacks of the frightful menagerie.

The noise in the store had become unbearable. It was near closing time, and the voices of the customers on their way out swelled to a deafening pitch as the human wave slowly moved toward the San Miguel exit. For a moment a woman rested her whole weight against my back, almost crushing me against the counter. I tried to pay and get out of there fast, but the chubby waitress didn't hear me. While I kept calling her, trying to make myself heard over the deafening noise, I thought of the years of poverty and hunger and recalled my aunt fixing a meal of soup for the famished ward heelers of the neighborhood and participating enthusiastically in their campaigns, believing, as did they, in a possible return to the feast they had lost forever, and eventually politicking herself, hoping only that the widower might be able to work again after all those years of enforced idleness. I remembered that during one fleeting interval of relative prosperity she acquired a massive dining room set that she immediately proceeded to hide under slipcovers, in preparation for a wedding that could not be far off. I took part in these preparations as enthusiastically as did she; but the wedding never took place, as my aunt, with her strange stubbornness, kept putting it off until she'd completed what she called her outfitting. I recalled the many scenes during which the widower threw his children out of the house, while the whole neighborhood would gather out in front and the rest of the family would shrink in humiliation.

And I recalled another occasion when they brought my aunt from a first aid station with her face battered from a fall. By that time she was having a hard time walking. Weeping indignantly, she complained there was no respect in the world anymore. As they'd helped her out of the car that had taken her to be treated, a voice, more solicitous than the rest, had risen from among that crowd of children that always turns up to watch any incident and had recommended, "Hey, hold her head down or she'll crack her old skull!"

Exasperated as I was by my vain efforts to make myself heard through the ever-swelling racket, I must have made a sudden movement, because the woman on my right drew away with a start. With all my heart I wished I could be left alone in that enormous place, as my aunt had been left alone when they made her move out of her home. When the owners of the old house, yielding to an offer from the Ten-Cen, sold the property, my aunt fell gravely ill at the prospect of an eviction. Slowly the rooms were emptied and their contents transferred elsewhere. Most of the lace-making machines were auctioned off because nobody made lace anymore; and away they went, along with the dining room set, the mint and basil in their flowerpots, the stored-away furniture, the widower's trunk, the photos of the dear departed, the moldy roses, and the rusty washstands.

All that was left in the huge empty house was the ceiba and the rosebushes that nobody had pruned in years, and my aunt in her room with its mirrored wardrobe, to which she alone had the key, its purple lamps, and its worm-eaten paintings. As soon as my aunt got well, the wreckers' pickaxe would come to demolish the house.

But my aunt never got well. The widower's children must have sensed she wouldn't, because suddenly they made their peace with their father and set themselves up as best they could in the half-empty house to defend his rights—or so they declared at the top of their lungs. My aunt was a long time dying. Outside, the pickaxe grew impatient while her illness and her dying slowly took their course. Those of us who were closest to her took up positions near her, taking turns at her bedside day and night in a kind of silent battle against the bestial tribe that was shouting outside, pounding on the walls and slamming the doors. As the end drew near and the intruders nearer still, we all felt a sense of duty and put aside our usual occupations to watch solicitously over my aunt's final moments, tacitly united in our determination to beat them to the key to the wardrobe.

The ruckus in the store reached an unbearable level and then suddenly ebbed as the mass of the customers spilled out onto the street.

One day when I came to relieve another relative in the sickroom, my aunt, paralyzed and unable to speak, looked at me with an expression of terror in her eyes, which had once been very beautiful and which over time had come to bulge. The widower entered the room; and when he left, the eyes focused on him and followed him till his shadow disappeared behind the glass door, and then turned again to me, almost bursting from their sockets to guide my attention to the wardrobe, which was closed. Then they looked at me again, and the head moved sideways. I shuddered. I looked at the wardrobe. It stood where it always stood, in the corner; but between one side of it and the wall there was a little gap. The eyes kept looking at me insistently. I went up to the wardrobe and I could see that at its back, barely concealed, one of the boards was resting on the floor. I pulled the wardrobe a little farther from the wall and then I saw that all the boards in back had been moved and that the inside was almost empty. The pieces of lace, the embroidered sheets, the great shawls smelling of camphor, were all gone. Only the old dresses were still hanging from their perches. With a violent effort I looked back at the face that was watching me from the pillow. One of the lamps was casting a pale glow onto the terrified and lightless eyes. My aunt was dead.

It was very late. The Ten-Cen was empty. The chubby waitress had left. A boy was washing the last cups of the afternoon, almost exactly on the same spot where her iron bedstead had stood. A little beyond where the ceiba had grown, two clerks were checking the day's receipts with an adding machine.

I felt the hard polished granite under my feet. I drank the rest of my cold coffee, paid, and left.

Translated by John H. R. Polt

Internal Monologue
on a Corner in Havana

Josefina de Diego

GOD, I'M DYING for a cigarette! If only my pension got me through the month, I wouldn't have to sell my rationed smokes. But a peso apiece, that's not bad, with that I can buy a little rice and a head of garlic every now and then. You can't do much on eighty pesos a month. Who would have thought that after twenty-plus years of work and with a university degree, I'd have to stand here on this corner selling my monthly cigarettes? And surreptitiously, because there's no way I'm getting caught in this "profit-oriented activity," as they say these days—without paying the tax on it I'd be in jail for sure. And how I love to smoke! But, in truth, I can't complain. This corner is quite entertaining, everybody's mixed up in something, more or less the same as me. Really it's a prime spot: the Farmers' Market and two kiosks of CADECA, the Houses of Hard-Currency Exchange. Such an ugly acronym, they really outdid themselves this time. There are other terrible, historic ones, like CONACA or ECOA, but this is one of the worst. Sometimes I miss potential customers because I'm amusing myself by people-watching. It's comical, almost musical.

You hear, "psst, psst, *change money*, listen, exchange," all the time, like a timid hawker's chant. Or else the old man who sidles up so mysteriously and tells you "I fix gas stoves" and keeps walking, and you don't know whether you really heard it or you imagined it all. The other day a lady let loose a really hair-raising yell because she thought the old guy was a thief, and then there was a hell of a fuss. The old man didn't show his face in the market for about a week. I could smoke this cigarette right now. God, how hard it is to quit! If it hadn't been for this illness, I'd still be working and things wouldn't be so tough. When they told me they were retiring me on eighty pesos for "total incapacity to work," I almost had a fit. What an absurd law, since when you get sick is when you have to spend the most. But all the letters I sent, complaining, didn't do a bit of good. That's the law. And eighty pesos, at the official rate, that's less than four dollars. So therefore: Improvise! Once in a while somebody with dollars drops a coin or two, which helps my budget out. The one who's even worse off than me is the guy who sells plastic bags from the *shopping,** for a peso. This truly is illegal, more illegal than what I do, because at least I bought my little cigarettes myself, but those bags, where did he get them from? Whenever I can, I warn him of possible inspectors. We have a kind of unofficial union of "you scratch my back and I'll scratch yours." We're all here for the same reason, trying to get by without hurting anybody much. In fact, it doesn't seem to me we're hurting anyone

---

* The *shopping*, pronounced "choppin," is Cuban slang for the network of hard-currency (dollar) stores, now accessible to Cubans and foreigners alike. The nickname probably comes from the bilingual ad for one such chain: *compras fáciles*, "easy shopping."

at all, but I can understand how the Government can't allow it. If everybody were like us—but no, people are too much, if you give them an inch they'll take a mile and they'll end up robbing you with machine guns like in American films. Boy, how I miss my TV! A few days ago it broke on me and now I can't even watch the soaps. Luckily just the picture went out, so at least you can hear it. 'Cause getting it fixed, forget it, it's Japanese, Sanyo, and the repairman charges in dollars. At least my nephew is an electronic technician and soon he'll be back from a mobilization in the countryside— he went with the university. The mobilizations of the sixties and seventies, they were fun. Or at least that's how I remember them. Maybe it's just the "good old days" always seeming better, I don't know. I always thought they weren't very productive, especially the Sunday morning ones. "The important thing is attitude, *compañera*," they told me when I tried to demonstrate to the leader in question that between gas, snack, depreciation on the truck tires, oil, et cetera, the cost was greater than any possible income. "Professional vices," he told me. "Be optimistic. You economists think too much." In those days to buy a pack of cigarettes over and above the ration was just a peso and sixty centavos—shocking—and now they charge ten. What I'd love to do would be to buy a jar of that coconut sweet from the guy across the way there, but for a dollar? That's what I get for a whole pack of loose cigarettes, no way. Maybe later on, if I get some "reinforcements" from my sister who lives in Venezuela. Every now and then along come a few dollars that I sure can use. If I sell all these cigarettes I'm going to treat myself to a paper cone full of banana chips, for two pesos, two cigarettes, that's not bad. You can't always live in austerity, no sir, because "Life is a dream," as my high school literature teacher always used to say. Such a good teacher! He made us learn a few things by heart, to improve our vocabularies he said. I never thought I'd come to understand so perfectly the part about "when he turned his head/he found his answer on viewing/that another wise man was chewing/his discarded crust of bread." Around here there are tons of those wise men. But the one who's really worse off than me is the one who picks through the garbage dumpster in front of my house. The poor man, he doesn't know there's never anything of value in there—I give it a quick look every day. He ought to go to one by some embassy or near the hotels. Although it's not so easy, because those dumpsters have got their proprietors by now. If I don't sell these cigarettes soon, I'm leaving, because it looks like Noah's Flood is about to hit. And I'll end up with no banana chips. Yesterday one of my neighbors, in the building across the street, put a sign up on his porch: "Plumber—house calls." He must be dimwitted, how else can he fix plumbing except by making house calls? There's a lot of nuttiness, people are posting all kinds of signs, hilarious ones. Not to mention the names of the *paladares*.* Cubans have a certain nostalgia for small businesses and for advertisements different from the official ones, which sometimes makes you want to cry: "The Delights of Eden," right, and what you see are three little tables with a few homemade tablecloths. But clean, and with pleasant staff.

---

* *Paladares*, literally "palates," are small family-run restaurants in people's homes. The popular term comes from the name of a fast-food chain started by a character in a Brazilian soap opera shown on Cuban TV.

I worked in one, and things were going really well, but then it got closed down and I was in the street again. Now it's started pouring, ugh, what do I do now? Smoke the cigarette and not buy the chips? A dilemma worse than Hamlet's! How would it go in my case, teacher? "To smoke or to eat, that is the question." That would be funny if it weren't the truth, and if weren't for the fact that this is me instead of some latter-day tropical Hamlet. Better I should take the cigarette home and, if there's gas, make a little coffee and have my smoke. As they say in that charming English movie, "Life isn't perfect and besides, it's short." Tomorrow's another day. Who knows, maybe a few bucks from my sister will turn up.

Translated by Dick Cluster

My Heroic Birth

Zoé Valdés

ACCORDING TO MY MOTHER, it was the first of May, 1959. She was nine months pregnant and already knew I was a girl. She walked and walked, she says, all the way from Old Havana to the Plaza de la Revolución to hear the Comandante. And in the middle of his speech I started to raise such a ruckus in her pelvic region that she thought her bones would break. They had to carry her out on their shoulders to the Quinta Reina clinic. Before she could make her way through the huge crowd, however, as she passed the speakers' platform, Che himself draped a Cuban flag over her belly. She hardly noticed, because I was putting her through such hell. All the while, Fidel was going on and on with his speech, his rhetoric denser than a forest of palm trees. And I kept kicking, elbowing, butting my head, trying any which way to escape from her body.

Her belly sagged all the way down to her pubis. It felt like an explosion of constellations inside her, she says. She closed her eyes and savored the pain of expectation. My father arrived, covered from head to foot in a layer of red dirt that he was trying to dust off, his palm-leaf hat pulled down over his eyebrows, his machete still in his hand. They had gone to get him at the sugarcane harvest. He crouched next to her belly and trembled when he saw the flag. When she told him that Che himself had put it there, he almost fainted with pride. He stuck out his chest, smiled with satisfaction.

She says that at that moment she was no longer sure what she was feeling were labor pains. Maybe it was just a stomachache. But after so many contractions, she realized that it couldn't be just some minor body function. Her body was taking on a whole new dimension, alternating between the microscopic and the macroscopic. Her intimacy was exposed to its limits, like some mathematical equation. She was a step away from the flickering Void. And so much life inside! My father, a bundle of nerves, swore over and over again that he loved her. Without him she could not have faced it. She pretended to be tough. She went into the bathroom and passed bloody, greenish stool. She spent the night whispering, over and over, "I'm going to give birth. This time I'm *really* going to give birth."

My father is forever reminding me how brave my mother was throughout her life. I was her first and only daughter. She was unaware—like every woman—how painful childbirth could be, and that unawareness made her defensive. She could never overcome her fear. They made her put on a ridiculous-looking hospital gown, short and low-necked, and had her lie down on a sweat-soaked hospital cot. They spread her legs. Now she would really find out about pain. The obstetrician ordered her to push with each contraction. He stuck his hand in, poked around, taunting her every push. The pain was like the pain of death. Life was beginning, but it felt instead like life was ending. My mother's waters hadn't broken, so they broke them with a long white plastic stick. A cascade of warm, sticky liquid spewed out, and this gave her courage. The specialist's hand shook her belly violently. There, where I am. Where I was.

They carried her over to a drab little room. Outside, my father was chewing his nails, pulling out his hair. He didn't even dare smoke. The walls of the room were gray with filth, the chairs as well, the two beds hidden behind folding screens. Every armchair held a moaning pregnant woman with bruise-covered arms hooked up to IV bottles. My mother waited with them, wasting away in a humiliating hospital gown, her belly still draped with the Cuban flag that Che had placed there.

Elena Luz, the guerrilla doctor, decided that though my mother was already dilated almost three inches, her contractions were too far apart. They hooked up an IV to her arm, which had been tanned by the sun during the demonstration and the Workers of the World Day parade. My mother said she felt like a dissected cow, as in one of those Dutch still lifes. She could no longer control the rhythm of her labor pains. Doctors came and went, prodding her belly and sticking their strange hands inside her.

She walked back and forth between the armchair and the bed. The doctors told her to push hard. She was trying not to faint. Again strangers' hands pried opened her vagina and felt around inside. Her insides were like a turtleneck. Blood flowed from her everywhere—her clitoris, her anus; she urinated, emptied her bowels. Her body was at the mercy of the blasé mediocrity she saw in the doctors' gazes.

With unseeing eyes, she gripped her knees as hard as she could and then pushed, roaring like a lioness. One leg broke free from her grasp and knocked the IV bottle to the floor. They gave her a shot in the other arm. Once more the fierce grinding inside her, the indescribable pain. According to the experts, she was about to give birth; according to her, she was about to implode. They made her walk to the delivery room. Halfway there, a great ripping tore her from vulva to anus. My head!

She climbed onto the bed in the delivery room. One push: nothing. Another tremendous, three-dimensional push. My head was stuck. Then one final push, the most powerful of all, the one that made her a mother and me a daughter. Burning. Pushed to the edge of death. In that push, she says, Life and the Great Beyond became one.

"Could that be God?" She still wonders.

She wanted to watch me emerge from her body, and cried softly, like a cat purring. I was easy and slippery. I was detached from myself. I still am. My mother ceased being me. I ceased being her. They cleaned up her insides with icy water and showed her the enormous placenta, as beautiful as a piece of sculpture. It still hurt, like nothing and everything. They sewed her up carefully. She knew she was losing a lot of blood. How long would the pain of the life force go on? Cut off from her universe, I set out into my own. Her pain had ended. Mine had just begun.

My father was beside himself with joy, though he was also bitterly disappointed that I hadn't been born on May first. There I was, a tiny little lump slimy with maternal gook, wrapped in the Cuban flag, and already my father was scolding me for failing to fulfill my revolutionary duty.

"She should have been born yesterday! Two minutes! Missed by two minutes! I've been betrayed! She should

have been born on the first of May! I'll never forgive either
of them!" He lamented my lateness over and over again, his
expression nonetheless euphoric. The doctor tried to console him: "Don't be so upset, *compañero*. Today is also an
important day. It is the Day of the Madrid Uprising, the
Executions in Madrid—Goya's painting, remember?"

My father didn't know the first thing about Spanish
history—or about any other history, for that matter. Maybe
just a little about the war of independence against the
Spaniards. The only thing he was sure of was that the Yankees were his enemy and that his Revolution had been born
on January first and that his daughter had been born in the
spring, which here in the tropics amounts to the same thing,
because the weather is hot as hell at both times of year.

"What will you call the little girl?"

"Hmm . . . I'll call her Victoria. Better yet . . . yes, even
better . . . Patria! Patria's an original name! I'll be the father
of Patria! The fatherland! The father of the fatherland!
Carlos Manuel de Céspedes! The first man to free his
slaves! Now there was a man with balls!"

Deeply moved by his own words, my father began to sob
uncontrollably, believing himself glorious.

Translated by Sabina Cienfuegos

The Dark Night of Ramón Yendía

Lino Novás Calvo

RAMÓN YENDÍA AWOKE from a troubled sleep aching in every muscle. Worn out, he had slumped down over the wheel while the car was still moving, scraping the curb that separated the street from the vacant lot. On the other side a row of new houses huddled symmetrically together. Some were still unfinished; others were occupied by small businessmen and prosperous working men who had not yet found their place in the community and were therefore not too aggressive. Either by instinct or by chance, Ramón had come here to rest. He had spent four days away from home, sleeping in his taxi in different places. One night he had stayed at the taxi stand right in front of the Parados Bar, and it was there that his troubles had started. He had been afraid, but he had made an effort to control himself and to prove to himself that he could face the situation. He did not want to run, for he knew in a way that if you run you are sure to be followed—unless, of course, you have protection. Every minute of these four days had been like a sentence of death he had seen coming, taking shape like a thick cloud, growing claws. Ramón could not run away, he knew that, but perhaps he might remain, hiding or just waiting. After every earth-

61

quake someone is always left to tell the tale. It is a terrifying gamble, but then, life itself is a gamble.

Still, on the second night he went out into the outskirts of the city, and the following night he drove up in front of the house of a revolutionary he knew, though the man probably did not know him. "Maybe he'll want to ride in my cab," he thought. If the man did, then perhaps he might be able to weather the storm unnoticed. Somehow he felt that the storm had to come and that it would pass. His regular customers had already gone away; therefore there was something serious in the wind.

Having had no experience in these struggles, Ramón felt almost as if he had fallen into a maelstrom. Three years before, he had begun to drive a cab, and his first daughters had been born four years before—now there were three of them, all girls and all sick. His wife did what she could. She had found a job sewing hatbands in a factory, and she would tie the baby in her cradle and leave her while she was at work.

All through these four days he had only been able to slip into their house twice. They still lived on the Calle de Cuarteles in one room. The back door opened on the patio, the front door on the street. Estela had been longing for their own little home, even if it was only a shack. They could have got one in the new development for a down payment of one hundred pesos. They would have been able to save the money if their eldest, the boy, had not fallen sick and died in spite of their desperate efforts to save him. Now that Ramón had a good cab, which he rented for three pesos a day, they were beginning to get on their feet again. He longed for a car of his own, too, a Ford or anything. He had some good regular fares, and he stayed at the wheel fifteen hours a day. But then besides his own family he had to look out for Balbina, a fool who had had eight children by three different men. Everything was hard. The cab drank gasoline like water. It was a six-cylinder job, but he did not have the patience to wait his turn in the stand. Now, four days before, he had rented a new car from a different garage. He was a nervous man with big brown eyes, who sensed things long before anybody else was aware of them. Sometimes, even when there was no actual sign, he could see things coming. The other drivers laughed at him and called him a spiritualist.

On the night of the sixth he put his car away early and did not go back to the garage the next day. On the eighth he went to another, the Palanca, and hired a newer car. None of his usual fares was in the street any more. They, too, must have seen the cloud that was gathering. Every day for a year he had been driving them, and when all is said and done, they were all right, at least to him. Their voices were warm and human, and they seemed to believe in what they were doing. They did not make arrests; they were informers and nothing else. Ramón, too, had assisted them, had helped them out.

Now, today, the morning of the twelfth, his premonitions were more urgent, like something out of a painful dream. Until three o'clock in the morning he had been cruising the streets or waiting outside of dance-halls or cabarets. He had not had a bad day; in fact, as far as that goes, there had been nothing unusual about it. Before turning in he had stopped beside a lamppost near the Capitol and counted his take, which amounted to six pesos and change. Just then he felt that he was being stared at hard by a passer-by, a young fellow who looked like a college student and who had his hand in his jacket pocket. Ramón decided to go home with the money; he made a detour and stopped a block away from the house. He walked up the side street, crossed the patio, and entered cautiously. He turned on the fine flashlight that one of his regular customers had given him, and played it as though he was a burglar or a policeman instead of a fugitive. Not that anything as yet implied that he was a fugitive, he just sensed it. He did not dare to switch on the electricity lest he make a target of himself, and he felt his way in. He turned the flashlight on the beds. In one of the cots the twins were sleeping naked, cheek to cheek on top of the sheet, with their open hands over their shoulders. In the second cot slept Estela and the baby; the empty one was his. No one awoke. Estela had on a nightgown, and her head was between her hands, which were turned palms up. In spite of all she had gone through, she was still beautiful. She was young; she had a delicate nose, large eyes, heavy hair, a strong chin, thick, well-formed lips, and a large, sensual mouth. As he stopped for a moment to gaze at her, Ramón could visualize her healthy, slightly protruding teeth, her honey-colored eyes, and her lively glance. Then he put the money on the table where his dinner was waiting for him and went out. There was nobody near the automobile. Everything seemed normal except that there were too many cars moving too fast and the lights were on in several houses. That was all—but it was enough!

On his return trip he passed police headquarters. There seemed to be an unusual amount of activity going on inside, and as he went by he thought the two sentinels on duty moved their guns nervously when they heard his car. He turned into the first street on the right without stopping to think whether it was a one-way street. He stopped at the next corner, in doubt about which road to take; his thoughts had turned back several years, and old scenes flashed before his eyes as if on a movie screen. In those days some sort of revolutionary spirit had taken hold of him; he couldn't say why, for he had never been able to examine his feelings coldly and analytically. Perhaps he had merely caught it from the air, for he did not read much and he did not belong to any group from which he might have absorbed any basic principles or which might have helped him to clarify his own ideas. Twelve years before, he had come with his brothers and sisters from the country. His father had lost his savings when the bank crashed and had disappeared into the swamps with his head held high and his body as stiff as a corpse. (Nobody had seen him since.) He had caught it without warning; it was in the air. The girls had not yet been born, and the little boy was strong and handsome. Ramón did not find business too bad, for he was lucky at picking up steady customers; perhaps it was because he was a good driver; he knew when to speed and when to go slow.

And that's how things were. Almost every day he picked up three or four young fellows, sometimes together and sometimes alone. He had not yet found out who they were; he only knew that they were revolutionaries and they had money to spend. Being a revolutionary was a virtue, for the word recalled the country's struggles for independence, and since childhood he had heard it constantly from people of all classes. It was the national bona fide currency. Therefore it was all right. Things were not so bad at home, and his customers were fond of him, for he seemed to them to be reliable. They would talk to him and gradually he caught their tone, their language, and their enthusiasm. He talked like them at the taxi stand, in the garage—in fact, almost everybody was beginning to talk the same way. There still did not seem to be much danger in it, and a fellow was not afraid to speak his mind and even to pay an occasional brief call late at night. Sometimes he served as a courier, driving his empty car from one place to another. They paid him regularly, and the pay was not bad. After all, Ramón was one of them.

Then the tide turned. Justino, the boy, got sick. Estela was pregnant and irritable. Then came the twins, hard going, and perhaps doubt. Ramón could get excited and carried away, but he lacked conviction. He saw that being a revolutionary was not all smooth sailing. One night—a night like this, at the beginning of August, near morning—two men hailed him. He realized at once that something was up. Perhaps they were plainclothesmen. Others had hailed him in the same way and then, when they were in the car, had said: "Police headquarters." When they reached the station he would discover that he had been charged with going through a red light or speeding or some such thing. Naturally, it was against the law, but the union would bail him out, and sometimes a judge was good-natured enough to let him off without fining him. These two men were not paying passengers, either; they also said: "Police headquarters," but this time, when he got there, he was given different treatment.

He stood it the first time. They took him into a bare room with the cement floor and walls splotched with blood, and they slapped him, punched him, kicked him. Not an insult or foul word but that they threw it at him; their language besmirched everything he loved; and they threatened that his wife would get hers, too. He took it all. Then, to his surprise, they took him to the front desk, and the lieutenant let him go. He got into his car and somehow managed to drive to the garage. He did not go home that night, for his lips were cut and he was spitting blood. He could say that he had had a collision; that was the excuse the police told him to give. No, thanks; he was not going home to his wife with any more trouble. During those days his best customers were in hiding, and his day's take did not amount to more than two pesos. He slept in the garage that night. Early the next morning he went home and told his wife that he had been out all night with a customer who said he would pay him later. One of the children was sick; the mother thought she was teething, but he was afraid that it was something else, for she cried all the time and was as thin as a candlewick.

During the days that followed he did not see any of his old customers, and he had the impression that eyes were watching him on all sides. That day and night he got two tickets, and the next day three. The fourth day he was taken back to the police station and beaten again, but this time worse. Then they let him go, but they assigned another cabby he knew to keep an eye on him and put him on the right track. He was a slippery fellow who worked at night, picking up fares in front of hotels and cabarets or waiting in taxi stands. He began his job with kid gloves; then gradually he began to put it into Ramón's head that politicians were out for themselves and looked out for nobody but number one. He told him some stories, and to Ramón the little room he lived in began to appear more and more gloomy and his family more anemic and pitiful. He struggled with himself before he gave in, but the other man's arguments were convincing. He told him that after all it was just a case of one politician fighting another. Didn't "they" have enough money to pay him? They all began in the same way, and they ended up by forgetting the people who had helped them up in the world. No, Ramón was a fool if he didn't switch sides. Naturally, he could continue to drive his regular customers, for he was only asked to follow certain instructions and get certain information.

That was the why and wherefore of it all. He was on a spot, and he gave in. They would wipe the slate clean, and he would be helped out. That was when Estela, trying to get the children back to health, began to dream about owning her own little wooden house, and he began to dream about driving his own cab. The doctor said the children needed fresh air and good food. It was always the same old story. Every worker's child needs fresh air and good food, but perhaps his would get it. After all, Ramón was human; unlike some other people, he had warm blood in his veins, and so he yielded for the sake of his family and for his own sake, too. And suppose he hadn't? Could he have let himself go on being arrested and beaten up? Could he have let Estela and the children die? He began to rationalize, for he knew that he was not doing the right thing, and it worried him so that he had to use all his willpower to go through with it. He calmed himself by recalling the goal that he had in view. Perhaps he had done wrong, but his motives were good. Should he have refused and let himself be wiped out?

From then on he hadn't had a peaceful moment. He lost weight, he became more nervous and gloomy, and he had to make a strenuous effort to hide from his wife the drama that was gnawing at him from within. He knew that some of the men he had informed on were in jail and that one had perhaps even been murdered. When he thought about it, his only consolation was that he was poorer than anyone else; all the others, at least, had relatives and friends who could do something for them and would never forget them. But there was nobody to lend him a hand. He could depend only upon himself, himself alone. If the day came when he did not take home his three pesos, his family would not eat; if he did not pay his fee every day, he would lose his car; if he got sick, he would not even be able to get into the hospital. So it was only right and human for him to take care of himself, no matter who had to suffer for it. He was always having to recall these arguments to quiet his conscience, but deep down inside he carried his own accusation, which tortured and pursued him. Every day his spirits sank lower, and he felt that sooner or later something was going to snap. The atmosphere was getting more oppressive; his best customers had disappeared, and he suspected that the others had begun to be suspicious of him. In fact, he was even afraid that he might be assaulted and he began to go about armed, feeling that he was engaged in the struggle. He always kept his Colt within reach; the feel of it had a quieting effect upon his nerves.

Finally he began to feel that he was being deserted by the very men who had got him into this—the other driver and the two or three plainclothesmen. They had enough to do to take care of themselves, and besides he was not much use to them any more. All the revolutionaries' doors were closed to him, and he felt paralyzed, as though he could not go forward or backward. After some months of this tension, he felt that he could not endure it much longer. When he saw the storm gathering and spreading, he had a sensation of relief. "Let's get it over with," he said, and he waited.

But soon this feeling of relief, which had been caused by the changed situation, gave way to a new kind of anxiety. He had the impression now that he was surrounded, cut off, blockaded even; he knew that somewhere, sometime, he was being sought for by eyes he might never even have seen, eyes that were perhaps just awaiting a more favorable opportunity that would soon come. Then the situation would be the same as that first time he had been taken to headquarters, only just the opposite; and this time it would take a more violent and decisive form. It would be the end— that's all. If they had found him out—he thought they had—and if the "new ones" won—and he knew they were winning—then there was no way out. There was only one thing to do: lie low and wait—or get the drop on them and defend himself.

Both solutions were bad. Now, while he was trying to make up his mind where to go, he wondered whether there might not be a third possibility. He had imagination, but he had no faith in the images he conjured up. Still, he had to make up his mind one way or the other. They wouldn't do anything to Estela; she was not to blame. The worst that could happen would be that she would have to face worse poverty, the children might die, maybe she would, too. . . . But if he saved himself, he would come back for her some day. Could he save himself?

He thought so. He started the car and let it roll slowly, though he did not know exactly where he was going. He thought he would take it to the garage and from there he would get to the country on foot or somehow. In Nuevitas there were still people who would remember him, or at least his father. They might give him some help, hide him, and let him wait. But then it suddenly occurred to him that there was sure to be a general uprising and that to appear in a little town would only be a sure way of attracting more attention, and that town was not revolutionary-minded. He had only a few friends there, as poor as he, whereas here in Havana at least there were plenty of people, plenty of houses. He would move to another garage! And if he could only move into a different house! That was what had been in his mind when he had gone over to that row of houses opposite the vacant lot, where they were building, but then he had suddenly felt utterly exhausted, and had fallen asleep before the automobile had quite stopped.

And now he was waking up on this August morning, when all hell was popping. Ramón realized that there was nothing he could do any more.

Two men with revolvers at their belts were going into one of the seemingly empty houses. At the same time another man came to one of the frameless windows, and when the others who were downstairs motioned to him, he rushed down. He, too, was armed. Ramón, who had got out of the car, had his head under the hood and was pretending to fix the motor. He did not know any of them, but they might know him. The three men, however, walked briskly up the street with a satisfied air. In normal circumstances they would hardly have dared to act like that, for Ramón was sure that they were revolutionaries and that they were going after someone. They were not workers like him; they were well dressed, though at the moment coatless, and they looked well fed. It was their fight, a fight between the top dogs. Why had he been dragged into it, first by one side and then by the other? Still, that's how it was, and now there was no way out. First the old gang had been going to get rid of him, and now the new one was going to finish him off. That was a fact.

Well, perhaps it was, and yet he still had a flicker of hope, though he did not know exactly why. At any rate, he was not going to give up his taxi for a while, and he was not going to put it in the garage. He still had enough money for eight gallons of gas. His first thought was to explore the roads running out of the city, but when he reached the highway he could see that in Aguadulce it was being patrolled. He turned at the first corner and dived back into the city.

There was excitement everywhere. The whole town was on strike, and the streets were full of people and cars crowded with civilians and soldiers. They were shouting, cheering, leaping about, and brandishing their pistols. Ramón put down the flag of his meter, but it was no use. Four respectable-looking men rushed out of a house on San Joaquín and into his car, ordering him to take them to the Cerro. At Tejas he saw a man struggling to get away from some others who had seized him and who were being egged on by the watching crowd, both men and women. Ramón took advantage of an opening in the mob to try to keep on going, but someone glanced into the car, and a group of men began to follow him, shooting as they came.

One of the bullets went through the back window and out through the windshield. Ramón stopped and his passengers jumped out of the car and began to run madly through the side streets, pursued by several youths. Among them there were some who were little more than children—one of them must have been about fifteen—but they were firing large revolvers. Ramón pulled over to the curb, thinking: "Now they are going to come for me," but nobody seemed to pay any attention to him. Some excited bystanders came up to him to ask where he had picked up his passengers, and when he had told them the truth, they ran off toward San Joaquín Street. He even gave them the number of the house the men had come out of, but perhaps they did not live there; most likely they had spent the previous night hiding in one of the stairways. Who could tell what would happen now to the people who lived there? Everybody was armed; everybody was looking for someone to shoot at.

Once more Ramón started the car and went back to the same place, saying to himself, almost aloud: "I'll get lost among them, and they'll think I'm one of them. That should throw them off the track." After all, he had been one of them. But then he wondered whether he could keep his nerve. He looked at himself in the mirror and saw that he was pale and unshaved like a fugitive. At a time like this his face alone would arouse suspicion. But then as he was passing Cuatrocaminos, he saw another group of men running by with guns in their hands; some of them were as bearded and as grimy as he. Doubtless they were men who had been hiding these last months or who had been freed from jail. He might give the same impression; at any rate no one would take him for a person who had been on the payroll of the fallen government. He kept on moving. A few blocks farther along he ran into a mob that was chasing a lone man. He was zigzagging madly down the street, hurling handfuls of bills at his pursuers, who did not stop to pick them up, but stepped on them and kept on following him, shooting as they went. Ramón waited with interest to see what the outcome would be. Finally the man, who was already wounded and had been leaving a trail of blood behind him, fell on his face a few steps from where Ramón had parked. On seeing that he had fallen, one of his pursuers went over to Ramón with his revolver in his hand and ordered him to give him a can of gasoline. Ramón obeyed, siphoning it from the tank with a tube. Seizing the can, the others sprinkled the wounded man, who was still writhing, while a third set fire to him. Ramón turned his back on the scene.

The streets were full of civilians and soldiers. Ramón started his car again. A few yards farther on, some armed youths piled into it and kept him driving them around for hours without any apparent objective. Sometimes they would get out, force their way into a house, and come out again. As they passed the garage to which his car belonged, he noticed that it had been broken into. He stopped and asked to have the tank filled. Seeing that the car was full of armed youths, the attendant did as he was asked, and Ramón drove off with his passengers without bothering to pay. An hour later the young men had him stop in front of a tavern and invited him to eat with them.

It was past noon. Ramón sat down at the table with the strangers. It surprised him that not one of them had bothered to ask him a single question; apparently they took it for granted that he was one of them, that as an ordinary taxi-driver he could be nothing else. While they ate, the young men talked mysteriously and with great excitement. They ate fast and went out into the street, apparently forgetting all about him, for instead of getting into the cab again, they went off down the street and disappeared into the crowd, which was thicker in this zone than anywhere else. They were in the very heart of the city. Ramón got in behind the wheel and sat for a while, wondering what he should do. He was tired; he had gone so long without eating that his stomach no longer seemed to want food. And yet his fatigue could not outweigh his anxiety. Now he was fully conscious of being in a world to which he did not belong and in which, perhaps, there was no place for him. It would do him no good to pick up with anybody now; nobody would recognize a man with whom he had committed a murder unless they had been friends previously. In a few hours those youths he had been driving would not know him. Everybody seemed to be looking too high or too low; nobody was staring at eye-level. And yet, he thought, there might be an advantage in that, for the people seemed to be possessed of a mysterious, frenzied sense of well-being which would perhaps prevent them from keeping too close a watch.

Ramón came out of this daydream to see that a man was staring at him insistently from the opposite sidewalk. The man was watching him with a cold, attentive gaze whose meaning he could not understand, but he was sure that there was something behind it. Making an effort to overcome his nervousness, he got out of the car and as calmly and as naturally as possible pretended to look for something in the motor. He got in again, stepped on the starter without giving it gas, trying to give the impression that there was something wrong with the car (and that was what he was worried about), and then started off with a series of jerks. The man pulled a scrap of paper out of his pocket and jotted down the number of the license. Perhaps he was not sure. Ramón's may have seemed to him one of those faces we do not like, yet cannot recall at the moment exactly where we have seen them before. Otherwise, Ramón was sure, the man would have done something right then and there. He took for granted that his fate had been decided, mentally at least, somewhere, by people he did not know. To escape from the whirlpool seemed completely impossible; he did not even dare think of trying, for the mere attempt would have aroused suspicion. If there was any salvation, it was at the very heart of the maelstrom.

There was no driving down these streets. The whole city had poured into them. Ramón turned into a cross street and stopped when he arrived at the corner of the Prado, for it seemed a place where he would be inconspicuous. To keep people from trying to hire him, he let the air out of a tire and jacked up the wheel. Then he opened his toolbox and began to poke around in the motor. He took off the top and unscrewed the carburetor and a valve. Then he took out the other valves and began to clean them. He noticed that they were full of carbon, and when he got to the carburetor, he saw that it was dirty and almost stopped up. No wonder the car jerked and rattled. The work calmed his nerves a bit. He did not look at anybody or anything except the car, and therefore nobody looked at him. He had taken off his coat, and in the trunk he discovered an old coverall that might almost have been put there on purpose. He put it on and smudged his face with grease. Then, climbing into his seat, he looked at himself in the mirror as he stepped on the starter. He thought it would be hard for anyone to recognize him the way he looked unless they scrutinized him very closely and knew whom they were looking for. Still, some of his features were hard to forget. His eyes were large and clear and tight-lidded. Above one of his high cheekbones there was a small scar, and the curious line of his lips made him look as though he was on the point of smiling—a wry smile. "Rabbit-laugh" they called him in the garage. All in all, his features made a strong impression. It had never occurred to him that this was of any importance.

He got out of the car and went on tinkering with it. He took out the battery, cleaned the terminals, and put it back again. When he had reassembled everything, it was getting late in the afternoon. Those hours had passed less disagreeably than any other time since the beginning of the strike. The work had quieted his nerves, and the car was running better than ever before. Checking the four inner tubes, Ramón saw that they were new; he had oil and gasoline. Before starting he took the revolver out of the pocket of the front door and examined it; it was a new Colt; with it he had a box of bullets. He took out those in the drum and snapped the trigger six times to make sure it was working right. When he had closed it again, he noticed that two or three boys were watching him enviously. Any one of them would have given his eyeteeth for a gun like it. The revolutionaries seemed to them the luckiest beings in the world. And they would be thinking that Ramón was one.

The car started again. Without knowing how he got

there, Ramón soon found himself a block away from his home. He stopped. He felt an irresistible impulse to run in, to pay them a little visit; but at that moment he saw a huge crowd coming down the cross street. They were bearing trophies and shouting cheers and threats. The trophies were scraps of curtains, bedcovers, pictures, a telephone receiver, vases. . . . Ramón did not wait to see any more, but dived into the nearest grocery and turned his back on the crowd. When the people had passed, he raised the hood again and said to one of the children who came over to watch: "Go to Number 12 on that street and tell whoever you see to come over here for a moment." The child charged off, happy to have been noticed, and was back in a couple of minutes to say that there was nobody at home. They must have gone over to Balbina's, Ramón thought. Estela must have realized—as much as to say: Estela knows that I am a dead man and has gone to consult with Balbina about how she's to look after the kids.

Once more he started the automobile. He went aimlessly along the same street as far as the Avenida de las Misiones, and there he turned off toward the sea. But he turned back at once, afraid of straying too far from the downtown area. He felt that as soon as he got to a solitary spot he would be assaulted, and there would be no witness to what happened. But what good were witnesses any more? None at all; but Ramón did not want to die, to be murdered, without someone around to tell the tale. It did not matter if they could not come to his aid; the deed would at least be engraved on their eyes, in their memories, and in a way it would stand as an accusation. Once at his house a crazy relative of his wife's had said: "Murder will out." She could not have been very crazy if she was able to say such deep things.

The sun was setting when he got downtown again. He moved slowly through parks and boulevards crowded with shouting, running people, and officers and soldiers fraternizing in a tremendous sense of triumph. All the cars were in motion; people and vehicles moved in whirlpools from which strong currents of vengeance emanated. He heard shots high in the air; everybody had bloodshot eyes, everybody was hunting something. That was what frightened him most: in everybody's eyes he could see the hunting instinct. The slightest reason, the slightest justification, would have been enough to unleash the rage he saw in every eye. As night fell, the movements of the crowds seemed to take on a new objective and a definite aim. There were groups that marched in brisk time, cutting like tanks through the others, which were shapeless and yielding. Ramón saw at once that these were like-minded comrades who felt they had a self-assigned mission to accomplish.

These last few days he had often wondered what had become of Servando, the driver who had started him off as a traitor. He had stopped going to the taxi stand; he had left his car, which was his own, in the garage, and Ramón knew nothing about him. Now Ramón was parked in the very stand that used to be Servando's. Cruising about aimlessly, he had stopped there, though he could not have said why or how. He had seldom stopped there in the past. A big wagon appeared along the street where the trolley ran. It was apparently loaded with sacks of sugar; the lone carter was driving a team of old, worn-out mules. As it came opposite the taxi stand, a group of eight or ten youths came out of a doorway and, going over to the driver, forced him to pull up. They began to throw the sacks on the pavement; after they had unloaded a number of them, three men climbed out from under the rest. The three men leaped to the pavement and shot off in the direction of the Prado. One managed to reach the first group of people and disappear; the second turned down the next street, closely followed by some of the youths, who were firing point-blank at him; Ramón did not have time to see the end. The third dropped right where he was. He had hardly touched the sidewalk, making for the doorway, when he straightened up suddenly, spun about on his heels, and toppled over. Looking out of the car window just as the man turned around, Ramón saw that his face was a mask of terror. It was Servando.

By then it had become completely dark. The people had begun to drift away, and there remained only the few who seemed to be going somewhere. Ramón at a glance could distinguish between the two kinds of people: those who were going somewhere and those who seemed to have no place to go. The latter withdrew early, leaving the streets to the others. "Now there's only them and us left," Ramón thought. Still he lingered for a while in the stand. He was the only one there; now he no longer dared to move away, for the center of the city was all open, while the streets were lined with dark doorways and sinister corners. The die was cast, he thought. Servando had fallen first, and now it was his turn, for his offense was the same. These maddened people were in no mood for explanations: they would not ask what his motives had been; they would only ask whether he was Ramón Yendía. The ghosts of the men he had betrayed would soon rise up to haunt him.

His train of thought was interrupted by the sight of a lone pedestrian who had stopped on the corner and was looking at him suspiciously. Servando's body had already been dragged away, and there was no longer any activity in the place where the car was parked. The pedestrian crossed the street diagonally, passing the car and looking at Ramón out of the tail of his eye as he went by. As he stepped up on the sidewalk, his face was illuminated by the light inside the building, where some factory hands were moving spools of paper. Ramón recognized the face instantly. It was that of one of his earliest (and less important) customers. He had been among the first to disappear when Ramón turned informer. This was bad luck, definitely. And now he was the first to turn up again. He would be followed by the others who were still alive. They would surround him. Perhaps they were already waiting for him at the street intersections he would have to cross. They had him cornered, like a runaway slave whose roads of escape have been cut off, and soon they would set the hounds on him.

Which hounds? The one that had stared at him as he passed must have been one of them, he was sure. A few moments later another man—a stranger, this one—passed and also stared hard at him. Ramón understood now that the executioners had arrived and that the execution ground would be that two-block rectangle. In his mind's eye he could see them posted, gun in hand, on the six corners. What were they waiting for?

This thought spurred him to action. He would not stay there. He would not accept death without a fight, huddled behind the wheel. At least he would run, fighting with what strength he had left.

Once he had made the decision, he stepped on the starter and set the car in second. Thinking only of his driving, he moved down the first block at a good clip. The mounting speed and the hum of the motor brought him a sudden feeling of complete relief. His anguished thinking was over; a sense of action took its place. The danger, the torment, the foreboding disappeared, leaving only one thing: the determination to run the gauntlet of his enemies and win out. As he approached the intersection where he supposed they would be waiting, he drove with one hand. In the other he held the revolver at the level of the window. But to his surprise no one bothered him, no one was waiting for him. He kept on a little farther along the street with the car tracks, and then slowed down. There were few people on the sidewalks, and they seemed to pay no attention to him. No one, not even his probable executioners, would believe that a condemned man could be at liberty and driving an automobile. Still, those men had looked at him meaningfully, and one of them definitely had a score to settle with him. Why hadn't he attacked him right then and there? Perhaps because he was not a killer; very likely he was not made of that kind of stuff. There are men who can't do it, no matter what they feel. There are some who can't even give the order. This man must have gone off with the information, and the other probably had nothing to do with Ramón.

Ramón pulled up beside a lamppost in the park. As he looked up toward an illuminated sign, he saw a clock. Time had passed too fast. Absorbed in his own drama, he had not felt it go by, and now it was nine. Now there was no one on the street except those who had something to do. You could see it by the way they acted and walked, but no one paid any special attention to him, though it seemed that everyone was hiding or at least betraying a certain amount of suspicion. Of all the cars that were moving about the city, his was the most conspicuous. He reflected that if it were parked, it would be likely to attract still more attention.

Then began a slow, painful drive. It seemed to Ramón that these were the last hours of his life, and that very soon, perhaps before daybreak, everything that his eyes could see and his ears could hear would have disappeared, dissolved into eternal nothingness as if nothing had ever existed in the world, as if he himself, Ramón Yendía, had never been born, as if all that he had loved, suffered, and enjoyed had never had any reality. And the scenes of his life began to flash before him in pictures, as on a screen, clear, sharp, and exact, neither hurrying nor lingering. Present reality itself took on a meaning that it had never had; it was the reality of a dream. In it he saw many things at the same time, and still they never ran together or became confused. Past, present, people, things, feelings—everything was sharp, transparent, and definite. And yet all passed in a kind of procession from which no detail was omitted. The streets were fairly empty, and not a traffic policeman was to be seen. As Ramón drove, the car might have been moving on rails or floating in the air. Without knowing why, he went to all the places most closely connected with his life. First he passed the house where he and his two brothers and two sisters had spent their first night in the city, Balbina's home. Then the little factory where Balbina worked, and from there to the house where his elder sister, Lenaida—what could have become of her?—had lived with the Spaniard. After that he drove past the house of the Chinese who had married his sister Zoila, and, forgetting that the city limits might be policed, he reached the outskirts—the little wooden shack where the baby had died. He had met Estela in that neighborhood, first at a dance and then behind the place where they had the cockfights. Where the dance-hall had been, there was now a factory; a watchman with a rifle stood at the door. Nobody bothered Ramón as he drove by. In fact, the soldiers who were guarding the exit from the city let him pass, once they had checked to see there was no one else in the car. On his way back, they did not even search it. Once more he passed the familiar places—the theaters, the movies, the nightclubs, the brothels, all those places where he had taken people looking for a good time. It had never occurred to him to think that life really had so many charms. Could it be on account of these charms that men fought and killed one another? And yet they were not satisfied; they always wanted more; they wanted to rise, trampling on others, just for the sake of rising and not merely in order to enjoy such things as music, women, wine, leisure, flattery, service, fine food, health—health!

This thought suddenly brought him out of his reverie. His car was moving along as though driving itself. There were no obstacles or stops; no one crossed the road; furthermore, he had been driving for five years, and now he could have kept it up all day long through the heaviest, most nerve-racking traffic, without having to think once about what he was doing; he could spend hour after hour musing and dreaming, letting his fancy wander, and still observe all the traffic regulations. Now it was easier. Then, suddenly, he began to concentrate on one thing: his wife and his children. It was for them, after all, that he had done what he had done, that he was where he was now. Where was he? He realized that he was just going by police head-quarters, the place where he had been "persuaded" to change sides. Without noticing it, he had passed within a block of his house, and now he was going up Montserrate Street. At the door there was a cluster of soldiers and civilians, and there was evidently a lot going on inside. He slowed down a little to come to another decision: he still wanted to go home and see whether Estela had come back and how the children were. He would leave the car a short way off; right around the corner, opposite Palacio, was a good place.

Before he reached the corner where he planned to turn, a car sped by, almost scraping his mudguard. A face peered out of the window. It was like a powder-flash. The face had appeared only for an instant, and it had been barely visible by the light of a street lamp, but that was more than enough. Ramón thought of going straight on and went into second at once, but before he could do so, the other machine, which was newer and faster, had cut him off. Then he went into reverse, made a sharp turn, and shot off at full speed in the direction of the sea.

And thus the chase began. The other machine, which was one of the latest models, started after him with the same fury. Two other new, fast cars started at once in support of the first, taking a shortcut through different streets, disregarding the one-way arrows. Ramón had recognized that face, but before he had even been able to start off, two bullets had whizzed by his ears. It was strange, but he was not afraid: no one had ever before shot at him from such close range and yet what he felt was not fear. Nor did he even feel distressed. That meeting had suddenly dissipated the terrible anxiety that had been oppressing him. His bursting brain, which had been pulled in a thousand directions, tortured by a thousand wires, began to work lucidly and with a single purpose. Like the aviator engaged in combat at an altitude of a thousand feet, he had only one objective: to overcome his enemies, even if it was only so that he might feel he had got the better of them. Before he reached the sea, the first Ford had caught up with him; they had managed to keep him within range and directly ahead of them. The three or four occupants at once opened fire with rifles and revolvers, but none of the bullets hit either the tires or the driver. One of them just grazed his skull; he had crouched down instinctively. As he emerged into the avenue, he pulled out the choke, turned the car rapidly, and gradually gave it all the gas he could. Then he took his foot off the brake and concentrated completely on the wheel and the accelerator.

The other car kept tailing him. Seeing the two of them turning in the distance, another of the pursuers cut out as he reached the Paseo del Malecón a few blocks farther down, but there Ramón turned right and went up the Avenida de las Misiones. Although he did not have time to think it out, he knew that he had the advantage on the turns. He had always been outstanding in the races for his skill on sharp curves. He would let up on the gas at the beginning of the curve and then suddenly, as he reached the end, give it all he had. Besides, he was a condemned man, fleeing for his life, and the dangers involved in speeding were of small consequence. His first pursuer also turned quickly and fell in behind, determined not to lose sight of him. Then the race began through the downtown streets. On reaching the Parque Central, Ramón shot like an arrow into the old city, where the narrowness of the streets gave him the advantage. And then in that labyrinth which he had covered a thousand times he was able to maneuver continually and throw the other cars off the track. Of course, Ramón did not have time to figure all this out. He, the man who had been so absorbed in thought, had suddenly burst into action under the guidance of a hidden being within him who had taken control. Seeing that he was going down Obispo, one of the other cars tried to take a shortcut through a side street on the assumption that he would turn to the right. The reasoning was correct, for two or three blocks farther down, Ramón turned right on a cross street. Hearing him coming, the other car attempted to block the way, but Ramón was speeding so fast that the other went up on the sidewalk and ran head-on into a wooden door, bursting into a brothel. This one was out of the race, at least for the time being.

The other two continued in hot pursuit without yielding an inch. Only by turning continually could he manage to keep out of their line of fire. They saw him for a moment from far off and began shooting, but he had just arrived at an intersection, and he turned quickly. The tires shrieked along the asphalt. Sometimes he took his foot off the accelerator for a moment, at other times he stepped on it hard, heedless of the danger. Even at a distance people realized that it was a race and got out of the way. One man climbed a lamppost like a cat the moment Ramón emerged into the Parque Cristo and—to quote the man—"turned like lightning" in the direction of Muralla Street. Somehow or other

the third pursuing car also foresaw that Ramón would try
to come out near the Terminal and sent two or three other
cars to cut off that exit. But before Ramón got there, the
shadowy being who was now guiding him made him turn
about. He went down San Isidro at full speed, turned into
the Alameda de Paula, went up Oficios, then along Tácon
and came out at the Avenida del Malecón. Now he had
another idea, and it was not to avoid the shots of his pursuers in narrow streets. It had suddenly occurred to him that
if he got into the open country he could jump out of the
car, leave it in motion, and flee through the hills.

But he could not get out into the hills by driving along
the wide streets where he would be an easy target, so he
turned at once toward the downtown section of the city, and
then, going uptown from there, he started to look for a way
out. Now he was being followed by two cars, which, however, were still unable to overcome their initial handicap.
Their advantage lay in their armed strength and numerical
superiority, and in the fact that if one ran out of gasoline,
the other could still keep on going. Ramón, on the other
hand, could not stop to fill his tank; perhaps that was why
he made up his mind to flee to the hills.

After weaving in and out of the streets for some minutes,
he decided to make a try for it. The moment had come
when he would have to go through some broad street for a
fairly long stretch. It was a risk he would have to run. His
first plan was to go down the Avenida de Carlos Tercero in
the direction of Zapata, past the cemetery, and then race
down beyond the river. But before he had finally decided
on this road, a strange idea came to him out of nowhere: he
would not flee into the country, but would go as far as the

hospital, run the car against a lamppost, and then enter the hospital to have his wounds bandaged. If he did not have a wound by then, he would inflict one on himself. Maybe his pursuers would not follow him so far, but would seek him instead among the houses where they found the auto. At the same time he thought that perhaps when day came he would find some way out. He did not know exactly how or what, but in some vague, indistinct way he still hoped to find it. Naturally, he was not sure whether the hospital was not also in the hands of those who were now his enemies.

Having worked out his plan, he decided to put it into effect at once. In one moment he visualized the exact spot where he would crash his car, and the speed that he would have to be making in order to put it out of commission and yet escape with his life. The thought of the hospital came to him purely by accident. Passing a street corner where he had run over a child years before, he remembered that he had taken him to the hospital; it had been one of the most agonizing moments of his life. While he was waiting for the doctor to operate, he had turned so pale, his face had become so distorted, and his eyes had taken on such a terrified expression that another doctor had taken one look at him and ordered some medicine for him which he did not recognize. After that they had taken him into a room full of strange white machines and examined his heart and asked him a lot of questions. To their surprise, Ramón was not ill, nor had he suffered any attack; his conscience was responsible for the expression on his face. The doctors themselves had asked the mother of the child, who, fortunately, did not die, not to be too hard on Ramón in her complaint. She was a very poor woman, and she did not even lodge any complaint; after that Ramón used to go to see her when he could and bring her a little present. He had always remembered the doctors' attention as one of the happiest experiences in his life. And now in this moment of supreme peril, when he had put his whole being into this struggle to save himself, he thought about those doctors or others like them as his possible protectors.

So he made a supreme effort to reach the hospital. As he was still in the heart of the uptown section of the city, he would have to cross a wide square before he could reach the place where he hoped to crash the car. Veering continually, cutting sharply, and turning on two wheels, he finally managed to approach his goal, but just as he was about to emerge into the broad avenue, he saw that two cars were drawn up across the street ahead of him. They were probably parked there. Ramón put on the brake as slowly as possible, mounted one of the sidewalks, and made a U-turn. The ones in front began to shoot at him; one of the bullets pierced his left wrist, but he felt very little more pain than if it had been a pinprick. As he turned, he observed that his inevitable pursuer was coming toward him like a torpedo and shooting as he came. The bullets hit the car, but none managed to put it out of commission. Ramón gave it all the gas he had and drove straight at the other. For a moment a fatal collision seemed inevitable; the pursuer saw Ramón's car coming toward him and jammed down the brake just before coming out of the street next to the last. Without reducing his speed, Ramón turned into it through a hail of bullets. The pursuer lost a couple of seconds before he could get up full speed, but Ramón had been hit by another bullet, this time right on the temple. It had scraped the skin, like a plowshare turning up the grass cover of the earth. It did not hurt, but the blood forced him to close one eye, which began to smart. And so, blind in one eye, with one wrist perforated, bleeding profusely, he continued the race. He kept up his speed, more determined than ever to reach the hospital. Once more he headed in that direction, but this time by a different road. With the slight advantage that he had gained, he was able to reach the Calle de San Lázaro; turning into it, he pushed the accelerator down to the floorboard and shot off in a straight line.

He was blocked again. From three cars that had been drawn up across one of the last intersections came a hail of bullets, but the shooting had begun too soon, and he had time to turn to the right and get out of the line of fire. But by now the first pursuer had been able to regain the time he had lost, and was coming straight at him.

Ramón was now headed toward the city along the wide Avenida del Maine. He had lost considerable blood, and with it, no doubt, some of the energy and mental alertness that made it possible for him to continue that uneven duel. He began to feel faint; his hand was trembling on the wheel. The car kept on down the middle of the avenue, but no longer as steadily as before. His pursuers noticed what was happening. Sometimes he would reduce his speed as if he was going to stop, and then he would hurtle forward at full speed. Furthermore, he was no longer traveling at a steady pace. Sometimes he would veer one way, sometimes the other, as if his steering gear was twisted. Three more cars caught up with the first pursuer. The quarry was losing speed. Now they had him!

Still fearing a trick, they did not close in at once. Surely there was someone else in the car besides the driver. If not, what were they following him for? One of the men in the first car assured the others that when the chase had begun he had seen a man throw himself to the floor of the taxi. Yet no one had answered their shots; there was only that crazy, desperately fleeing driver. Then he himself must be guilty; otherwise why expose himself to such danger? They followed him, no longer shooting, always keeping their distance. It was obvious that the pursued man was losing speed and control. Sometimes he appeared to be getting ready to stop once and for all, but then he would move ahead in a series of jerks. Now they had him within range not only of their rifles, but of their pistols too. With what strength he had left, Ramón once more reached the Avenida de las Misiones, and then for no apparent reason turned back toward the city. He kept coming back to the spot where both his home and police headquarters were located and where the pursuit had begun. His pursuers guessed that he was trying to make it to headquarters. All they could think of now was not to lose the man who, they supposed, was in the back seat. In order to make his escape impossible, the car on the left and the car on the right drew up almost alongside Ramón, while the one in the middle approached from behind.

Opposite the Palacio, Ramón's car almost stopped, but then it moved forward again briefly, as if in the tow of an invisible force. The others kept their distance, approaching slowly. Once more Ramón stopped, this time in the very spot from which he had set out.

The lights were still on in headquarters, and people were going in and out; the air seemed filled with a distant noise, a noise filtered and deadened through a dense felt wall. The different voices were merged into a single even, dying murmur. Ramón turned his eyes toward the building, whose inner lights were bursting from the windows. His head drooped over his left shoulder, went limp, and sank on his chest. And still there was that smothered, dying noise far away, very far away. . . .

The other three cars stopped side by side in the middle of the street. Several armed men jumped out; others came out of police headquarters and surrounded Ramón's car. One opened the front door, and the driver tumbled out over the runningboard with his feet still on the pedals. At the same time others threw open the rear doors and searched the inside with their flashlights. There was nobody there! Then one of the leaders bent over the driver, who was still lying with his body twisted, his head hanging, and his eyes closed. He flashed the light on him, looked at him slowly; he put out the light and reflected for a moment as though trying to recall something. Then once more he shone the light on the face and once more stopped to think. Everybody around him was silent, awaiting an explanation. The man said: "Does anybody know him?"

Nobody knew him. More men came out of headquarters. The body, still warm, was taken out of the car and carried inside. And in the electric light they were able to distinguish his features clearly. They were not ordinary features. Anybody who had ever known him would have recognized him. But no one recognized him. The first man who had shot at him was called in.

"What did you see in the car?" the policeman on duty asked.

"I am sure I saw a man; he looked out of the window and then he hid. Then I looked at the driver, and he tried to get away at once. That's why I followed him, and when we were out a ways he returned the fire."

They searched the car, but there was no gun. Ramón had not fired; most likely someone in one of the houses had done it. In fact, his revolver had been stolen from the pocket of the door, perhaps in the taxi stand while he was watching one of the men who was staring at him so intently. No one had seen anything else. The only testimony was that of the boy who thought he had seen a man in the backseat. But why had the driver fled? He was only an ordinary hacker, obviously of no importance at all. They looked at his license, they inquired of the Secret Police and the Justice Department. They could not find his name in any of the files. Meanwhile the body was there, lying on a table. They had taken for granted that he was dead, though he was really only in a state of shock due to loss of blood. But in two hours his body was rigid and cold. His address was on his license; a policeman went to his house, woke Estela and asked her some questions, but got nothing. The terrified, trembling woman could give them no information. She was living in the greatest poverty; it was impossible that a government agent could have been so badly paid.

All who had taken part in the pursuit were now standing perplexed around the body. Why the race, the pursuit, the victim? No one could throw any light on anything. If there had been a passenger, he could never have jumped out of the car. There had been no opportunity, for he had never been traveling slowly enough, and they had never lost sight of him. As far as the driver was concerned, they had not been able to get to the bottom of things even in the garage. Everybody regarded him as a nice guy; nobody had ever heard that he had any political connections. (Obviously they did not consider him very important, for the only person who had known anything about him was his boss, the other driver, and he had been silenced forever. He had left no written evidence, for he carried everything in his head.) Finally, near dawn, there appeared a little man in uniform who had once been a policeman and was now a clerk. He shouldered the others aside and stood staring thoughtfully at the corpse. Then he looked around while he stroked his long, tobacco-stained mustache.

"Why did you kill this one?" he asked. "He is one of your own men. I remember him. I don't know who he is or what his name is, but quite a while ago I saw him brought in here and beaten up. They said he was a revolutionary. And he must have been one of the best. They took him in there two or three times, and they beat him black and blue, but they couldn't get a word out of him. Then he never came back."

They looked at each other. The old man turned around, once more shouldered his way through the crowd, and went back to his work, bowed by the weight of years and experience.

Translated by Raymond Sayers

Máscaras

Leonardo Padura Fuentes

WHEN HE DISCOVERED that the nearly impossible address really did exist, Lt. Mario Conde closed the notepad in which he had copied a number of facts from the fat dossier on Alberto Marqués Basterrechea. He stuck the pad in his back pants pocket and gazed at the bougainvilleas, miraculously joyful under the unforgiving two P.M. sun. The magenta, violet, and yellow flowers merged like magic butterflies into a tangle of leaves, spines, and branches that seemed capable of surviving any disaster on a local or worldwide scale. A few palm trees with arrogant, luxurious tops shaded this garden and gave a rather somber cast to the house, set a few yards back, which indeed was number seven on Calle Milagros between the cross streets of Buenaventura and Delicias. Could that number and those names be a trick on the part of Alberto Marqués? To locate his house in such a corner of the Earthly Paradise, at the intersection of miracles, good fortune, and delights? Yes, that had to be one of the infinite strategies of the Evil One, because the reports Conde carried in his notebook indicated that anything might be expected from the clever and diabolical Alberto Marqués. The security specialist responsible for the Ministry of

Culture had handed him the old but still healthy dossier with a splendid smile. Marqués was a preying homosexual of great experience, politically apathetic and ideologically deviate, a problematic and provocative individual, bearer of foreign influences, highly cultured, difficult to fathom, a possible consumer of marijuana and other drugs, a protector of stray queers, a man of doubtful philosophical affiliations, full of petty bourgeois and classist prejudices, all noted and classified with the evident aid of a Muscovite manual that detailed the techniques and procedures of socialist realism. This impressive resume was a compilation of the written, summarized, correlated, and even cited-to-the-letter remembrances of several police informants, successive presidents of the local Committee for the Defense of the Revolution, cadres of the ancient National Cultural Council and the contemporary Ministry of Culture, the political advisors of the Cuban embassy in Paris, a Franciscan monk who had been the subject's prehistoric confessor, and a pair of his perverted lovers interrogated in strictly criminal cases. "What the hell am I mixed up in?" Conde asked himself.

He tried to clear his mind of prejudices. In vain, he thought as he crossed the garden and climbed the four steps to the front door, "because I love prejudices, and I can't stand queers." Conde pushed the bell that stuck out like a nipple below the number 7. He caressed it twice, and then again, because from outside he couldn't hear any ring or buzz. When he was about to push it again, or maybe to make use of the knocker, he felt that darkness was assaulting him. The door slowly opened alongside the pallid face of the playwright and director Alberto Marqués.

"What am I accused of now?" the man asked. His deep voice had an explicitly ironic tone. Conde tried to take in stride the door which seemed to open by itself, the spectacular whiteness of his host's face, and the question which was his opening surprise attack.

He opted for a smile. "I'm looking for Alberto Marqués."

"You have found him, Mr. Policeman," the man said, opening the door a few inches wider, as he might raise a curtain, to give Conde the forbidden pleasure of seeing his whole body in that space. It was not so much pallid as colorless, thin to the point of being squalid, the head barely crowned with limp and bodiless fuzz. He was wrapped from neck to ankles in a Chinese robe that might have dated from the Han dynasty. At least two thousand years of suffering, the policeman thought, must have been inflicted on that cloth. Its colors were as faded as the man's face, the silk ripped and roughened so it seemed nothing like silk, and covered with battle scars in the form of stains that might be coffee, bananas, iodine, or even blood. The garment of illustrious emperors had come to a most sad and irregular state.

Conde made an effort to smile, remembering the terrible reports now pressed against his rear. He ventured to inquire, "How do you know I'm a policeman? Were you expecting me?"

Alberto Marqués blinked a few times and tried to organize the limp remnants of his hair.

"It doesn't take Sherlock Holmes. In this heat, at this hour, with your face and at my house, who would be coming but the police? Besides, I know about poor Alexis."

Conde nodded in agreement. This was the second time

in recent days that he'd been told he had a policeman's face, and he was inclined to think it was true. If there were bus-drivers with busdriver faces, doctors with doctor faces, and tailors with tailor faces, it wouldn't be hard to look like a policeman after ten years on the job.

"May I come in?"

"Might I keep you out? . . . Come in," he added finally, opening the door into darkness.

Inside the heat was gone, even though every window was closed and there was no sound of any electric fan. In the cool dark room Conde could just make out a steeply pitched roof, and some scattered pieces of furniture as dark as the space itself, which was large and divided into two parts by a pair of columns whose heights might be Doric, or not. In the rear, some fifteen feet away, there was a hallway, equally dim. Without closing the door, Alberto Marqués went to one of the walls and opened a french door, which spread harsh August sunlight onto the checkerboard floor, creat-ing an illumination both aggressive and unreal—like a spot-light directed to a given point on the stage. Then Conde understood everything. He had happened upon the set of *The Price*, the Arthur Miller play which Alberto Marqués had staged thirty years ago with such great success that it was still remembered today and, in addition, certified in his security file. Some ten years back, Conde himself had seen a revival under the direction of a most faithful disciple. Now he found himself on the stage where the characters would enter, of course . . . but could that be?

"Please sit down, Mr. Policeman." Alberto Marqués pointed with reluctance to a caoba wood chair darkened by years of fossilized sweat. Only then did he close the door.

Conde made use of these few seconds to take a better look. Between the floor and the hem of the man's robe he could see two sharp and skeletal ankles, as translucent as his face, that extended into a pair of bare ostrich feet that ended in strangely fat and separated toes with grooved nails like claws. His hands, by contrast, had a pianist's elongated fingers. And the smell? With a nose devastated by twenty years of tobacco, Conde tried to separate the odors of dampness, cooking oil, and something hard to classify while he observed how the man in the Chinese silk robe settled himself in another armchair, opened his legs, carefully placed his skeleton's hands on the wooden arms as if he wanted to embrace them, possess them, and finally bent those very fine fingers around the front curves of the wood.

"So, the floor is yours."

"What do you know about what happened to Alexis Arayán?"

"The poor soul . . . That he was killed in the Bosque de La Habana."

"And how did you find out?"

"I got a phone call this morning. A friend had heard."

"What friend is that?"

"One who lives around there and saw the commotion. He asked what was going on, he found out, and he called me."

"But who?"

Alberto Marqués sighed heavily, blinked some more, but didn't move his hands on the arms of the chair.

"Dionisio Carmona is his name, if that's what you're asking. Are you happy?" He tried to make clear that the confession bothered him.

Conde thought of asking for permission, but he told himself no. If Alberto Marqués was ironic, he would be rude. How did that faggot dare to treat a policeman this way? He lit the cigarette and blew smoke in the direction of his subject.

"You may drop the ashes on the floor, Mr. Policeman."

"Lt. Mario Conde."

"You may drop the ashes on the floor, Mr. Policeman Lt. Mario Conde," the man said.

Conde obeyed. The fucking fairy won't get away with anything with me, he thought.

"What else do you know?"

Alberto Marqués shrugged his shoulders while closing his eyes and heaving another dramatic sigh.

"Well . . . that he was strangled. Dear god, the poor creature."

Perhaps the man was really upset, Conde thought. And so he attacked.

"No, technically he was asphyxiated. Pressure was applied to his neck until he ran out of oxygen. With a red silk sash. Did you know he was dressed as a woman, all in red, with a shawl to boot?"

Alberto Marqués had let go of the arms of the chair, and with his right hand he was stroking his cheeks and chin. Touché, Conde concluded.

"As a woman? In a red dress? A long one like a very old-fashioned gown?"

"Yes," Conde answered. "What do you know about that? Because as far as I know, he left this house to go there."

"Yes, he left here yesterday about six, but I swear I saw him a little before, and he wasn't dressed as Electra Garrigó."

"Electra Garrigó?"

"I designed that dress myself, on my first and last trip to Paris, for my version of Virgilio Piñera's play, which was supposed to premiere in Havana in 1971 . . ."

This faggot is trying to pull the wool over my eyes, Conde was thinking, when he realized his bladder wouldn't let him wait any more. The tale of Parisian transvestism which Marqués had spun in pursuit of the red dress in which his boyfriend had been murdered bore too much resemblance to a fable invented for the purpose of trapping the unwary in a spider's web. And later swallowing them— perhaps intellectually, or perhaps physically, such as if, for instance, they said they needed to take a leak. Crossing his legs only made Conde's urge worse, increasing the pressure on a vessel swollen by all the liquids he'd ingested to fight off the heat. He understood that he had only two options: either to ask the theater director for the use of his bath-room, or to leave. The second solution was as bad as the first. He wanted neither to establish any kind of relation-ship with this character, nor to let go of such a valuable guide into the sordid mysteries of Alexis Arayán's double life. This dried-up Marqués was his primary witness, per-haps even the murderer of that man who'd worn a mask. Although—he thought while turning to study the physical appearance of his host in the hopes that distraction would keep him from pissing his pants—would those skinny, seven-month-old's arms really be capable of strangling any-one? But going to the bathroom in someone else's house had always seemed to Conde to be the first step toward some kind of intimacy. Seeing what was in their bathroom was like observing a piece of their soul. A pair of dirty underwear, an unflushed toilet, or a tube of scented bath gel could be as revealing as a confession before a priest. Or a judge.

"I have to go to the bathroom," he said then, almost without having so ordered his brain.

He expected Marqués to smile. Marqués did. And he leveled at Conde a look which made him feel measured, weighed, and prodded in his most intimate spots.

"Right over there, third door on the left. Oh—to flush it you need to hold up the handle until the water carries off all the outflow, if you know what I mean."

"Thanks," Conde said and stood up, knowing that his bladder had betrayed him in a most annoying way. He advanced toward the dark hallway and then through two rooms. Since he was within Marqués's line of vision he barely looked to either side, but he could tell the first was a bedroom and the second a study, full to its high ceiling with books. Then he discovered the source of the smell he hadn't been able to identify before. It was the oppressive and magnetic perfume of old paper, humid and dusty, and it wafted from a closed-in room, equally dark, that had to be the library of Alberto Marqués. Populated, surely, by works and authors excluded according to certain codes—and by exotic marvels unimaginable to the common reader, though Conde tried to imagine them with the residues of intelligence which weren't occupied in worrying whether he'd make it to the toilet or not.

He opened the door and found the bathroom. Unlike the rest of the house, it seemed clean and orderly, but he didn't take time to study it. He stood before the bowl, revealed his desperate penis to the light, and started to feel all the relief in the world flow toward the floor. It flowed and flowed while he glanced toward the door and thought he saw a shadow through the frosted glass and a poorly inserted patch. Was Marqués peeping at him? Conde covered his penis with his hand, watching the door while he finished up. That's all I need, he thought as he shook himself and welcomed the uncontrollable spasm of the end of the expulsion. He quickly replaced his diminished member inside his pants and flushed the toilet according to the instructions he'd received. Farewell, outflows, he thought to himself.

When he emerged from the hallway he found Marqués seated in his armchair in the living room. Conde approached him and sat down.

"It's so nice to pee when one needs to, isn't it?" the director asked. Conde was sure he'd been observed. Motherfucker, that's the limit, he thought, but he tried to seize the offensive now.

"What do all these stories about Paris have to do with Alexis Arayán?"

Marqués smiled and let a few short whimpers escape.

"Excuse me," he said. "Well, it has to do with the dress they found him in, and to do with the fact that he wasn't a transvestite. Better put, he wasn't what you'd call a practitioner, though at times he'd do it as a game. He'd dress up and perform characters, both female and male, but he'd never have been capable of going on stage, if you know what I mean. He was too shy and cerebral, too full of inhibitions. Am I making myself clear? But he always liked that dress very much. Although Alexis was homosexual, as you must know, I never thought he'd have the necessary daring to be a transvestite. As far as I know he never went out dressed in women's clothes."

"So why did he do it yesterday?"

"I don't know. That's what you need to investigate. That's what they pay you for, isn't it?"

"I believe they do," Conde said.

Translated by Dick Cluster

Thine Is the Kingdom

Abilio Estévez

SO MANY STORIES have been told and are still told about the Island that if you decide to believe them all, you'll end up going crazy, so says the Barefoot Countess, who is crazy, and she says it with a mocking smile, which isn't a bit surprising because she always wears a mocking smile, and as she says it she jingles her silver bracelets and perfumes the air with her sandalwood fan, on and on and on, sure that everyone is listening to her, and strolls through the gallery with her bare feet and her cane, on which she unnecessarily leans. She talks about the Island and with the Island. This is not an Island, she exclaims, but a tree-filled monstrosity. And then she laughs. And how she laughs. Listen, can't you hear it? The Island has voices, and indeed everyone believes they hear the voices because the Barefoot Countess's craziness is infectious. And the Island is a bounteous grove of pine trees, casuarinas, majaguas, yagrumas, palms, ceibas, and of mango and soursop trees that produce the biggest, the sweetest fruits. And there are also (surprisingly enough) poplars, willows, cypresses, olive trees, and even a splendid red sandalwood tree of Ceylon. And the Island grows a multitude of vines and rosebushes that Irene plants and tends. And it is crisscrossed by stone paths. And it has, in the center, a fountain of greenish water where Chavito has placed a clay statue of a pudgy little boy holding a goose in his arms. Forming a rectangle, houses arise, just barely managing to stem the advance of the trees. The trees nonetheless have strong roots and lift the paving stones of the galleries and the floors of the houses and cause the furniture to move, to wander as if they possessed souls. I tell you the day will come when the trees enter the houses, the Barefoot Countess insists in the tones of a prophetess. And though they feel afraid, Merengue, Irene, and Casta Diva laugh, they laugh at her, that crazy woman is full of surprises.

You get to the Island through the great door that lets out onto Linea Street, in a neighborhood of Marianao called (easy to see why) the Ovens. The entryway must have been sumptuous some years back. It has two severe columns supporting a pediment and a solemn, well-rusted iron gate that is always closed. High in the gate, next to twisted iron letters that read THE ISLAND, sits a bell. If you want them to open for you, you have to shake the gate several times to make the bell ring, and then Helena will come out with the key and open the padlock. The times are very bad, Helena says to everyone who comes, by way of justification. The visitor has to recognize that, indeed, the times are very bad. And go into the courtyard. No matter that outside, there in the street, the heat might be unbearable. The courtyard has nothing to do with the street: it's cool and humid, and it feels good to stay here a while and let your sweat dry. In one corner you can see Merengue's cart, so white it's a treat to look at, with windows that gleam. There are also different varieties of malanga growing in flowerpots, and a coarse reproduction of the Victory of Samothrace. You still can't see the Island, though you can feel it; from the courtyard you can't make out the Island because a huge wooden screen blocks your vision. Before you get to the gallery, the walls are a tarnished yellow, and the ceiling, supposedly white, is as yellow as the walls. The lamps are of unadorned iron, and hardly a one of them has its glass intact. In the first corner, right next to Uncle Rolo's door, sit a dark metal spittoon and a wooden hat stand that has eroded away, unused. When you get to the end of the wooden screen and take a few steps forward along the left side of the gallery, you can declare that at last you have arrived in the Island.

And no one knows exactly when the Island was built, for the simple reason that it was not built at any one time, but at many times over the years, as a function of Godfather's advancing or declining fortunes. The only thing that's known for sure is that the main entrance was built when Menocal was in power and the "fat years" were in full swing. Everything else is speculation. Some think the first house was Consuelo's, erected around 1880, and they may be on to something if you notice that Consuelo's house is the most run-down. Rolo asserts, using facts he draws from who knows where, that a good part of the construction was already standing when the Treaty of Paris was signed. A fact that's hardly worth remembering if you bear in mind that Rolo is capable, for the sake of appearing to know something, of asserting the most ridiculous nonsense. Whatever the case, it is evident that this enormous rectangle of stonework that encloses one part of the Island (the part they call This Side) was not erected all at once, but rather was built up through a series of changing tastes and needs. And perhaps that's why it has the improvised air that so many attribute to it, the feel of a building that has never been finished. High and irregular time-blackened walls. Scant windows of frosted glass. Narrow double doors. Blue and mauve skylights. Why put a date on it? Professor Kingston explains, with irony, that the Island is like God, eternal and immutable.

And it is fortunate that the houses are in This Side, because The Beyond is practically impassable. A narrow little wooden door, built by Godfather many years ago and now almost in ruins, divides The Beyond from This Side. The Beyond is a wide strip of open terrain running down to the river where only one house stands, Professor Kingston's, and one shed, where in another time Vido's father kept his carpentry shop. The only path through that area that you can more or less see is the one the old professor has worn with his daily walk.

It happens that, taken altogether, the Island (This Side and The Beyond) is many islands, many patios, so many that sometimes even the people who have lived there for years get lost and don't know which way to turn. And Professor Kingston states that it depends on the hour, because for every hour and for every light there is an Island, a different Island; the Island at the siesta, for example, is nothing like the Island at dawn. Helena maintains that without statues it would be a different place. That's true, the statues. Who could imagine the Island without statues? The statues with which Chavito has filled the Island. They are beings, mute and motionless but as alive as everyone else, with as much consciousness and poverty as everyone else, as sad and as weak as everyone else. So says the crazy woman. And the others smile, shake their heads. Poor woman. Poor, crazy woman.

In one little corner that no one sees, between the Discus Thrower and the Diana, heading toward Consuelo's old house, the Virgin of La Caridad del Cobre stands in a case built of glass and stones (brought back from a quarry in the province of Oriente). The stones and the glass blend in with the foliage. You have to know where the Virgin is to find her. She's a tiny, humble image, no pomp, just like the original in the sanctuary of El Cobre. Everyone knows that this Virgin is the Patroness of Cuba; few know that there is no image more modest, more diminutive (barely ten inches tall), without any involuted splendors, as if it were purposely constructed to be hard to notice. The (eminent) artist who sculpted her mixed-race face is, of course, anonymous. Her (unadorned) dress was cut from coarse cloth of a nearly white shade of yellow. She has no crown; to be sincere, she needs none: her sloe-colored hair is crown enough. The child in her arms, mixed race as well, has a delightful expression on his little face. And where the anonymous artist proved his greatness was in the three young men at the Virgin's feet, who row desperately in their boat, trapped by the storm over there toward the bay of Nipe. Everyone knows that La Caridad appeared to these three young men who were about to die. She chose them to be saved. She chose to reveal herself to them. Since they are so small, you have to look very carefully at them to discover that the anonymous (and eminent) artist has endowed them with life, that is to say, with anguish. Two of them (who have not yet had the Vision) are sure they are going to die. The third, however, the most chosen of the three, has already discovered the radiance and is looking up above. The anonymous artist has been able to depict him right at the moment when the shock has not yet gone from his face but blessedness has already begun to cover it. It should also be recorded here that the wooden wave that is trying to swallow the three men is a display of virtuosity. Before this humble (because of its size, I mean) image, Helena has placed an unadorned vase that she always fills with yellow flowers. There are, besides, a few votive offerings. Don't lose sight of the glass case, of the Virgin, almost lost among her pagan companions (the Discus Thrower and the Diana). At some point she will be the protagonist of a singular deed that will mark the beginning of the catastrophe.

Did you know the sea was near? Yes, it is near and there are few people who know it. I couldn't say why so few know that, since in this Island, no matter where you get lost, the sea has to be near. On an island the sea is the only thing that's certain, because, on an island, the land is what's ephemeral, imperfect, accidental, while the sea, to the contrary, is persistent, ubiquitous, magnificent, partaking of all the attributes of eternity. For an islander the perpetual discord of man against God does not play out between earth and heaven, but between earth and sea. Who said that the gods live in the heavens? No, let me tell you once and for all: both the gods and the devils live in the sea.

I couldn't say why so few know that the sea is near, since after you walk past the narrow little wooden door that divides This Side from The Beyond, and you go beyond Professor Kingston's room, Chavito's studio, the old carpentry shop; after you cross the ditch that they ostentatiously call the River (what zeal for ennobling all that is small, poor, coarse!), you enter a grove of marabú bushes. They call this wilderness Mount Barreto. (Barreto was a kind of tropical Gilles de Rais.) In this grove, toward the right, a little path opens up. Perhaps, I know, it is euphemistic to call it a path. It is simply a narrow space where the marabú isn't so aggressive, where with a little bit of imagination you can walk without undue difficulty. Walking through there for half an hour you get first to the ruins of the house they say belonged to Barreto (where they buried him, where they say he still lives, despite the fact that he died more than a hundred years ago). Then the marabú starts thinning out, the earth begins turning to sand, and the marabú trees give way little by little to pine trees, rubber plants, sea grapes. Suddenly, when you least expect it, everything comes to an end, that is, a strip of sand emerges. And the sea appears.

I have decided that today should be Thursday, late October. It has gotten dark long before dusk because today was the first day of autumn (which is not autumn) in the Island. Even though the sun rose on a beautiful summer day, little by little, so slowly no one could notice, the wind began to pick up and the heavens covered over with dark clouds that sped on the night. Chacho, who had gotten back from Headquarters just past four in the afternoon, was the first to notice the coming storm, and he told Casta Diva to take in the laundry that was hanging outside, and he went out to the gallery. The woman saw him later, absolutely motionless, watching perhaps the tops of the trees. It's true, Casta Diva thought, it looks like the world's coming to an end, and she shut the windows not just because the wind was strong, it also blew in sand and filth and raised up swirls of dead leaves. And you could hear the windows slamming shut. Irene, who had left for the plaza of Marianao just after lunch, found upon her return a layer of dirt covering the floor and the furniture, and some poplar branches embedded in the grillwork over the main window. At the foot of her bed, smashed to bits, was her porcelain pitcher. Irene bent down to pick up the pieces into which it had broken. One of the sharp corners of porcelain opened a small wound in her finger. It was almost five o'clock. At approximately the same time it grew so dark you had to turn on the lights. And Helena lit an oil lamp in front of the little image of Saint Barbara she always kept with the family photos. She did not do it mechanically like at other times, but with a certain devotion, and mumbling something under her breath. Sebastián saw her illuminated by the slim flame and he felt that her habitual solemnity was leaving his mother's face. Sebastián had been home early; Miss Berta had cut short the geography class to tell them that, since rain was imminent, the afternoon lessons were over. That was more or less the same time that Tingo-I-Don't-Get-It went looking for Sebastián, and that Merengue decided he wasn't going to make any more sales that day, since very few people would slow down to buy a pastry with this kind of weather brewing, and he left his spot at the entrance to Workers' Maternity Hospital. In reality, the storm was a pretext: he had a tremendous need to hole up at home. Mercedes got back from City Hall at the same moment Merengue opened the iron gate to let his pastry cart into the courtyard. When Mercedes went into her house she saw her sister in the shadows, the tip of her chin fallen against her chest. She ran up to her, thinking she had suffered another relapse of her illness. Marta pushed her lightly away. Why are you sitting here in the dark? Mercedes asked. Her sister smiled: Why should I need light? Is it raining? Mercedes said no, and let herself collapse in the other rocking chair and realized how tired she was. No, it isn't raining, but it won't be long before the downpour starts. And Melissa went out onto the terrace roof, holding Morales on one hand. She went out there smiling, happy at the inevitable arrival of the storm. From up high, from her privileged position, she spied Uncle Rolo in the gallery. It made her feel wicked to see that the foreboding storm did not make him happy as it had made her. And just as you might have expected, she laughed, laughed heartily, because that's how Melissa is and there's no understanding her. And Melissa was right: the afternoon had left Uncle Rolo feeling sad, or as he would say to excuse himself, it provoked "vague pains in his muscles and deep sorrows in his soul." Without closing the bookstore (was it really an oversight?) Uncle Rolo had gone out to observe the Island. At the exact instant Melissa saw him, he saw Lucio caressing the thighs of the Apollo Belvedere just behind the wooden screen in the courtyard.

Is it a lie to say the Island is like God, eternal and immutable? It had a beginning, it will have an end, and it has changed over the years. Is it also a lie that the main entrance was built when the fat years were in full swing, and that the first house was Consuelo's, and the nonsense that Uncle Rolo says about the Treaty of Paris? Lies. Fairy tales. False stories told to sow confusion. Legends. And as for the truth about the Island, who could say that they know it?

And if it is true that willows, cypresses, olive trees are not common in Cuba, why do they grow in the Island? Beautiful ones, every bit as good-looking as the yagrumas, majaguas, palm trees, and ceibas they grow next to. How do beeches, date palms, Canadian firs, and even a splendid red sandalwood tree of Ceylon grow there?

The lights are on in the galleries. For all the good that does. If today weren't today, Merengue would have taken a rocking chair out to the gallery as night began to fall, so he could smoke his H-Upmann and talk. Right away Chavito would have come out with his collapsible canvas stool and his shamefaced smile, and he would have sat down facing the black man, because there's no denying Chavito enjoys Merengue's conversation. Mercedes would arrive, bathed and dressed to the nines again, her neck and breast immaculate with all the Myrurgia talcum she poured on, and she'd lean against a column, sighing and saying with a smile that she comes there to forget for a few hours about City Hall and that damned Morúa. Casta Diva would arrive, with her hibiscus-print apron and her air of a diva, exclaiming, Please, don't tempt me, don't tempt me because I have so much to do. And Chacho would be following her, pretending to be upset, exclaiming with false anger, This woman! You just can't keep her in the house. Irene would come too, with her palm leaf fan and her smile. If it were a truly special night even Miss Berta would appear, since she is at times capable of taking a break in her prayers to forget that she is an exiled daughter of Eve, as she says with the perfect diction of a doctor of pedagogy. It's highly likely that Uncle Rolo would also be sighted, since there are nights when Rolo begins to draw near, as if against his will, as if he were a victim of chance, and he would bring with him (otherwise it wouldn't be him) his melancholy, his defeated appearance, and a half-urgent, half-hopeful gaze, as if the people who got together in the Island were all superior creatures. And Merengue, who knows him well, would sit there watching him with sorrowful eyes and exclaim to himself, though making sure everyone could hear, poor man, poor man. Guffaws would break out. The conversation would begin. (None of this happens: we are now in a novel.)

Today the evening lights went out too soon. Lord, let me dream. Very early, Marta closed her eyes. Give me, at least, the possibility of having my visions, my own visions. Her eyes lived scarcely by the light of day. Since I can never know the real Brussels, the real Florence, let me walk through *my* Brussels, *my* Florence. And she went into the house without turning on any lights; why should poor Marta with her eyes closed need lights? I would love to see tall mountains bordering immense lakes with castles and swans. Marta goes to bed. Or doesn't go to bed. There is a strong wind and it seems like people are pushing on the doors and windows. Since You have condemned me to the rocking chair, to this constant, dark, nearly black redness, give me too the possibility of *seeing* a ship, a street, a deserted plaza, a bell tower, an apple tree. Please God, I want to dream. Dream. Since I cannot see what everyone else sees, let me have access at least to what no one sees. It's so simple.

Translated by David Frye

The Messenger

Mayra Montero

THAT MAY there was a lot of lightning. The thunder was so loud it shook the walls, and there were little claps of thunder far away, like the footsteps of a devil walking round us.

My mother went to see José de Calazán, and I went with her to Regla. I waited for her outside the house, but through the open door I could hear their voices, the whispers of the *babalawo*, the sound of her crying. In their conversation they used some phrases in the Lucumi language, phrases that Calazán saved for difficult moments. Then they raised their voices and their talk grew stronger, their shouts grew louder, until they became tired, or their words turned into stones. Finally, they spit out those stones and lit cigars.

In the little boat that took us back to Havana, my mother said that my godfather had forbidden her to take Ester's picture out of the grave where it was buried along with Baldomero's bones. You couldn't give bones air, or light, or grief, and we wouldn't fix anything by troubling them. I felt relieved because I didn't like the idea of opening the coffin of a man I had once known as strong and blond, and finding only his bones. I didn't even know what color they would be. And I didn't feel brave enough to look at Ester's picture, at her face come back from dust and darkness, her expression after so many years. That made me afraid.

My mother said that in cases like mine, you had to turn to the power of the paisanos. She called all the Chinese paisanos, those who had been my father's friends and those who hadn't. One of the paisanos was Yuan Pei Fu, who used to sell fruit and in his old age devoted himself to cultivating his power: the power of the blacks mixed with the power of the dragons. The result of those two powers was a warrior surrounded by smoke: Sanfancón.

"Calazán can't do any more," my mother repeated. And what the black *nganga* can't do, the Chinese *nganga* always can.

Yuan Pei Fu lived in a house on Calle Manrique, just before Real de la Zanja, in the heart of Chinatown. Seven of his paisanos lived there with him, and my mother knew them all. Those Chinamen wouldn't look us in the eye, they mumbled when they talked or didn't talk at all, but they treated my mother like one of the family. There weren't any women in the house, and she acted as though it was hers: as soon as she walked in she began to straighten and clean, she would pick up the clothes and wash the dishes, change the sheets and hang up the clean towels she brought once a week because the Chinamen didn't own any; I wondered what they used before to dry their hands.

When I was a little girl, my father used to take me there too. He'd stay in one of the rooms, smoking, and I'd wander around looking at the Chinese lanterns. Yuan Pei Fu, who was the Great Olúo, the *babalawo*, the head brujo, would give me candies, and there was another Chinaman, a cripple, who cut little dolls out of paper and gave them to me to play with. When I turned fifteen, I had to bring an offering to Sanfancón, who was master of the sword and the thunder. To tell me the story of this saint, whose real name was Cuang Cong and who had lost his head in battle, Yuan Pei Fu would raise his arms and run around the house shouting, "My head! Where's my head?" Then he would squat beside me and tell me the sad part of the story that began on the Ship of Death, during the Twelfth Moon in the forty-seventh year of the Emperor Tu Kong. The ship was the 22 frigate *Oquendo*, and the date of moons and emperors was January 2, 1847. The day when more than three hundred Chinese left Canton to come to work in Cuba. Yuan Pei Fu was eight years old then, and he traveled with his father, who was the guardian of an image of Cuang Cong. At night the men would gather around the image, burn incense, and ask the saint to let them reach land safely. But that didn't happen, because a few days after they set sail the sickness broke out, cholera or typhus, and the men died on deck, gasping for breath and flopping around like little fish. They had to throw ninety-six bodies into the ocean, and Yuan Pei Fu's father was one of them, but before he died he told his son to take care of the image of Cuang Cong. After that, Yuan Pei Fu never let it out of his sight again, and he carried it off the ship when they landed in the village of Regla. José de Calazán, my godfather, hadn't been born yet, but his father, Moro Calazán, was in the crowd that came down to the docks to watch them walk off the ship. At first the people laughed: it was the first time they had seen Chinese slaves chained up like blacks, but even more ragged and desperate, with sunken eyes and their feet swollen with seawater. In the middle of all those men was a child, a little boy carrying an image that looked like Changó to the people of the Lucumi nation.

The saints are the same everywhere; they're the same in China and in Guinea. That's what José de Calazán and Yuan Pei Fu decided on the day my mother brought them together so they could talk. They met in Regla, in Calazán's house, and it was really an event because the Chinese *babal-awos* never met with the black *babalawos*. They drank their drinks, they talked about their *orishas*, and Calazán said it was a great coincidence that the scared little Chinese boy his father had seen walking off a boat had turned into such a wise and clever old man.

My mother said that for this reason, and for other reasons I didn't know and couldn't even imagine, my godfather, José de Calazán, would not be offended if we asked Yuan Pei Fu for help.

"The saints," my mother said, "are blood brothers. So are the *babalawos*. And you have the blood of a paisano."

She didn't mention it again, not even on the morning when she woke me just before dawn and told me to get dressed because we both had to pay a visit. We left Amargura and went straight to Calle Manrique. My mother was talking to herself, walking fast and looking down at the ground, and I thought she was practicing what she would say to Yuan Pei Fu. When we came to the Chinamen's house she crossed herself, took out her key, knocked twice, hard, the way she always did, and opened the door. It was dark inside, but my mother knew all the corners and rooms where the paisanos slept, two to a room except for Yuan Pei Fu, who had his own room and altar, and the cripple, who slept in the middle of the living room. At that hour most of the Chinamen were out, selling what they sold: the dried peaches they called "ears," little figures made of sesame seeds or roasted peanuts, and a fish that had black flesh whether it was fresh or salted, a disgusting thing that I didn't think was used for anything good.

My mother went straight to Yuan Pei Fu's room, pushed open the door without knocking, and pulled me in by the arm. The Chinaman was squatting in a corner, smoking or burning sticks of incense. You could hardly see anything there was so much smoke. Only the image of Sanfancón, above us, guarded by a circle of thick candles.

"The man is in Cuba," Yuan Pei Fu announced, his voice coming from a distant place, not his mouth or throat but somewhere up high, from the mist or the clear blue sky. "I've been seeing him for days."

I wanted to ask who he was talking about, who was the man who had come to us, and how did he see him, but my mother fell to her knees, raised her hands to her face, and looked as if she would burst into tears.

"He's very close," the Chinaman added, and then he went on talking in Cantonese. My mother raised her head and began to drink in those words, as if she understood them all. Yuan Pei Fu didn't say goodbye to me that day, he couldn't even smile or smooth my hair, which was his way of telling me goodbye. We left him sunk in that pit of mysteries, shaping strange figures with his hands, joining and twisting those slender fingers of his—in the dark they looked like worms to me.

Before we went back home, my mother wanted to go to the Church of La Merced and make an offering to Santa

Flora, the beheaded saint we always prayed to. We bought white flowers, lit a candle, and kneeled in front of the golden goblet that held the tongue of the virgin saint. My mother crossed herself and made the sign of the cross over me with holy water, bent her head and prayed, and after that prayer she seemed more peaceful. When we were back home we didn't talk about Yuan Pei Fu again, or the few words he had said to us.

The month of May ended quietly. Nothing unusual happened in my life, and when June started I felt relieved. My mother noticed this and warned me not to forget what Calazán had said, to keep it in mind no matter how much time went by.

One Sunday after lunch, I got ready to deliver some sewing we had finished on Saturday. Two of the parcels were going to the same house on Calle Compostela. The third had to go a little farther: to the Hotel Inglaterra. Of all the things that happened that day, the saddest was my mother's face when we said goodbye. She'd had a premonition and said she was thinking about my grandmother, who had come to her in a dream and talked to her from the other world in the Lucumi language. But the thing she had noticed most was that the whites of her eyes, which had always been yellow, had turned white again. My mother saw the change as a sign. We hugged and I went out. I delivered the first two packages without any problem, and sometime after four I walked down Paseo del Prado, turned onto Calle San Miguel, and pushed opened the little metal door to the kitchen of the Hotel Inglaterra. The cook was glad to see me; I gave her the package of clothes, and she paid me. Then she asked if I'd like something to drink, and though my mother and I usually didn't spend time chatting with our clients, I felt thirsty that afternoon and said I would. Two men were also working in the kitchen: one was washing pans and the other was peeling vegetables. The cook gave me a glass of lemonade in a pretty blue glass, but I hardly had time to raise it to my mouth when we heard a huge explosion. She shouted "Holy God!" and looked at the men, who ran outside to the street. I dropped the glass and took out my protection, a little bag that Calazán had strengthened for just this moment. I tied it to my hair and waited.

"It came from the theater," one of the men shouted. "The ceiling collapsed, a lot of people must be hurt."

I tried to leave, but the cook held on to me. She said I'd be safe there. The streets were full of commotion and screaming, and there might even be more explosions. I stepped back and leaned against the table where one of the men had just been chopping squash. I picked up a stringy clump of seeds, squeezed them, closed my eyes, and then it seemed I could hear the voice of Yuan Pei Fu:

"He's very close." I opened my eyes again and looked toward the street, toward the open door, and at that moment a man appeared in the doorway. Again the cook exclaimed "Holy God," and I began to whisper the litany my godfather had told me to say: "*Iyá nlá, Iyá Oyibó, Iyá erú, Iyá, mi lánu . . .* ," that's a prayer that means: "Great Mother, Mother of the whites, Mother of the blacks, have mercy."

The man rushed in, tore off his cloak, and dropped it on the vegetable skins scattered around the floor. All he wore under the cloak was a white tunic, and in that tunic he looked to me like a king from another time, a warrior *orisha* running from the fury of another *orisha*. I wanted to run, too, but I had lost my voice and my will and was thinking that my fate was sealed: the man who had come to crown me, the man who had come to die in Cuba, or who was dead already, marked and condemned by the saint in his own head, had come out of the smoke and the noise and finally stood trembling before me.

"Bring me a glass of water."

He said it with authority, and the cook hurried to give it to him. He looked around for somewhere to sit and found a stool beside me. He came toward me slowly, passing his hand across his forehead. On his head he still wore something that looked like a turban decorated with snakes, then he took it off and put it on the table next to the chopped squash. I could smell the odor of his clothes, I saw his sandals and his feet covered with soot: I think I began to love him because of the tips of those small toes that seemed like women's toes to me. Many days later, when we were far from Havana, I caressed those toes and confessed in a whisper that it had all started there, in the place where the Chinese *babalawos* say you can find the tail of the soul. He began to laugh and swore he could hardly remember anything about that afternoon: the explosion, the dust that had gone up his nose and down his throat, the horror he had felt because his throat was sacred. He couldn't even remember that the cook brought him a glass of water, and that before she gave it to him she recognized him and stepped back in a kind of daze: "Excuse me, Señor," she kept repeating, then finally she reacted and handed him the glass.

He drank the water and was quiet and thoughtful for a while, but suddenly he asked where he was. The cook told him he was in the kitchen of the Hotel Inglaterra, and he said he couldn't go back to his hotel, the Sevilla, and it would be better for him to stay in this one. He asked if the Inglaterra was safe, and that's when I remembered my godfather. I had the feeling that José de Calazán was standing beside me, whispering into my ear what I had to do, telling me that if I wanted to, if I took him away, the man wouldn't die.

"The Inglaterra isn't safe," I lied, "but I can take you to a place that is."

The cook looked at me as if she couldn't believe what she'd just heard, she stammered a few words that didn't change anything because he stood up right away and said: "Let's go." Then she took me by the arm. She was a good friend of my mother's and knew very well who José de Calazán was. That's why I told her I was going him to take him to my godfather, that Calazán himself had told me to do that. Nobody argued with Calazán's orders, least of all a woman, and so she didn't argue, but she was so bewildered she dug her nails into my arm. Her nails were short, but she had strong fingers.

"Aida, do you know who this man is?"

I knew and didn't know. He was Calazán's nightmare. And mine.

"Girl, that's Caruso!" And she pulled her hand away as if it had been burned.

Translated by Edith Grossman

Ocean Blue

Cristina Garcia

CELIA DEL PINO, equipped with binoculars and wearing her best housedress and drop pearl earrings, sits in her wicker swing guarding the north coast of Cuba. Square by square, she searches the night skies for adversaries then scrutinizes the ocean, which is roiling with nine straight days of unseasonable April rains. No sign of *gusano* traitors. Celia is honored. The neighborhood committee has voted her little brick-and-cement house by the sea as the primary lookout for Santa Teresa del Mar. From her porch, Celia could spot another Bay of Pigs invasion before it happened. She would be feted at the palace, serenaded by a brass orchestra, seduced by El Líder himself on a red velvet divan.

Celia brings the binoculars to rest in her lap and rubs her eyes with stiffened fingers. Her wattled chin trembles. Her eyes smart from the sweetness of the gardenia tree and the salt of the sea. In an hour or two, the fishermen will return, nets empty. The *yanquis,* rumors go, have ringed the island with nuclear poison, hoping to starve the people and incite a counterrevolution. They will drop germ bombs to wither the sugarcane fields, blacken the rivers, blind horses and pigs. Celia studies the coconut palms lining the beach. Could they be blinking signals to an invisible enemy?

A radio announcer barks fresh conjectures about a possible attack and plays a special recorded message from El Líder: "Eleven years ago tonight, *compañeros,* you defended our country against American aggressors. Now each and every one of you must guard our future again. Without your support, *compañeros,* without your sacrifices, there can be no revolution."

Celia reaches into her straw handbag for more red lipstick, then darkens the mole on her left cheek with a black eyebrow pencil. Her sticky graying hair is tied in a chignon at her neck. Celia played the piano once and still exercises her hands, unconsciously stretching them two notes beyond an octave. She wears leather pumps with her bright housedress.

Her grandson appears in the doorway, his pajama top twisted off his shoulders, his eyes vacant with sleep. Celia carries Ivanito past the sofa draped with a faded mantilla, past the water-bleached walnut piano, past the dining-room table pockmarked with ancient history. Only seven chairs remain of the set. Her husband smashed one on the back of Hugo Villaverde, their former son-in-law, and could not repair it for all the splinters. She nestles her grandson beneath a frayed blanket on her bed and kisses his eyes closed.

Celia returns to her post and adjusts the binoculars. The sides of her breasts ache under her arms. There are three fishing boats in the distance—the *Niña,* the *Pinta,* and the *Santa María.* She remembers the singsong way she used to recite their names. Celia moves the binoculars in an arc from left to right, the way she was trained, and then straight across the horizon.

At the far end of the sky, where daylight begins, a dense radiance like a shooting star breaks forth. It weakens as it advances, as its outline takes shape in the ether. Her husband emerges from the light and comes toward her, taller than the palms, walking on water in his white summer suit and Panama hat. He is in no hurry. Celia half expects him to pull pink tea roses from behind his back as he used to when he returned from his trips to distant provinces. Or to offer her a giant eggbeater wrapped in brown paper, she doesn't know why. But he comes empty-handed.

He stops at the ocean's edge, smiles almost shyly, as if he fears disturbing her, and stretches out a colossal hand. His blue eyes are like lasers in the night. The beams bounce off his fingernails, five hard blue shields. They scan the beach, illuminating shells and sleeping gulls, then focus on her. The porch turns blue, ultraviolet. Her hands, too, are blue. Celia squints through the light, which dulls her eyesight and blurs the palms on the shore.

Her husband moves his mouth carefully but she cannot read his immense lips. His jaw churns and swells with each word, faster, until Celia feels the warm breeze of his breath on her face. Then he disappears.

Celia runs to the beach in her good leather pumps. There is a trace of tobacco in the air. "Jorge, I couldn't hear you. I couldn't hear you." She paces the shore, her arms crossed over her breasts. Her shoes leave delicate exclamation points in the wet sand.

Celia fingers the sheet of onion parchment in her pocket, reads the words again, one by one, like a blind woman.

Jorge's letter arrived that morning, as if his prescience extended even to the irregular postal service between the United States and Cuba. Celia is astonished by the words, by the disquieting ardor of her husband's last letters. They seemed written by a younger, more passionate Jorge, a man she never knew well. But his handwriting, an ornate script he learned in another century, revealed his decay. When he wrote this last missive, Jorge must have known he would die before she received it.

A long time ago, it seems to her, Jorge boarded the plane for New York, sick and shrunken in an ancient wheelchair. "Butchers and veterinarians!" he shouted as they pushed him up the plank. "That's what Cuba is now!" *Her* Jorge did not resemble the huge, buoyant man on the ocean, the gentleman with silent words she could not understand.

Celia grieves for her husband, not for his death, not yet, but for his mixed-up allegiances.

For many years before the revolution, Jorge had traveled five weeks out of six, selling electric brooms and portable fans for an American firm. He'd wanted to be a model Cuban, to prove to his gringo boss that they were cut from the same cloth. Jorge wore his suit on the hottest days of the year, even in remote villages where the people thought he was crazy. He put on his boater with its wide black band before a mirror, to keep the angle shy of jaunty.

Celia cannot decide which is worse, separation or death. Separation is familiar, too familiar, but Celia is uncertain she can reconcile it with permanence. Who could have predicted her life? What unknown covenants led her ultimately to this beach and this hour and this solitude?

She considers the vagaries of sports, the happenstance of

El Líder, a star pitcher in his youth, narrowly missing a baseball career in America. His wicked curveball attracted the major-league scouts, and the Washington Senators were interested in signing him but changed their minds. Frustrated, El Líder went home, rested his pitching arm, and started a revolution in the mountains.

Because of this, Celia thinks, her husband will be buried in stiff, foreign earth. Because of this, their children and their grandchildren are nomads.

Pilar, her first grandchild, writes to her from Brooklyn in a Spanish that is no longer hers. She speaks the hard-edged lexicon of bygone tourists itchy to throw dice on green felt or asphalt. Pilar's eyes, Celia fears, are no longer used to the compacted light of the tropics, where a morning hour can fill a month of days in the north, which receives only careless sheddings from the sun. She imagines her granddaughter pale, gliding through paleness, malnourished and cold without the food of scarlets and greens.

Celia knows that Pilar wears overalls like a farmhand and paints canvases with knots and whorls of red that resemble nothing at all. She knows that Pilar keeps a diary in the lining of her winter coat, hidden from her mother's scouring eyes. In it, Pilar records everything. This pleases Celia. She closes her eyes and speaks to her granddaughter, imagines her words as slivers of light piercing the murky night.

The rain begins again, softly this time. The finned palms record each drop. Celia is ankle deep in the rising tide. The water is curiously warm, too warm for spring. She reaches down and removes her pumps, crimped and puckered now like her own skin, chalked and misshapen from the saltwater. She wades deeper into the ocean. It pulls on her housedress like weights on her hem. Her hands float on the surface of the sea, still clutching her shoes, as if they could lead her to a new place.

She remembers something a *santera* told her nearly forty years ago, when she had decided to die: "Miss Celia, there's a wet landscape in your palm." And it was true. She had lived all these years by the sea until she knew its every definition of blue.

Celia turns toward the shore. The light is unbearably bright on the porch. The wicker swing hangs from two rusted chains. The stripes on the cushions have dulled to gray as if the color made no difference at all. It seems to Celia that another woman entirely sat for years on those weathered cushions, drawn by the pull of the tides. She remembers the painful transitions to spring, the sea grapes and the rains, her skin a cicatrix.

She and Jorge moved to their house in the spring of 1937. Her husband bought her an upright walnut piano and set it by an arched window with a view of the sea. He stocked it with her music workbooks and sheaves of invigorating Rachmaninoff, Tchaikovsky, and a selection of Chopin. "Keep her away from Debussy," she overheard the doctors warn him. They feared that the Frenchman's restless style might compel her to rashness, but Celia hid her music to *La Soirée dans Grenade* and played it incessantly while Jorge traveled.

Celia hears the music now, pressing from beneath the waves. The water laps at her throat. She arches her spine until she floats on her back, straining to hear the notes of the Alhambra at midnight. She is waiting in a flowered shawl by the fountain for her lover, her Spanish lover, the lover before Jorge, and her hair is twisted with high combs. They retreat to the mossy riverbank and make love under the watchful poplars. The air is fragrant with jasmine and myrtle and citrus.

A cool wind stirs Celia from her dream. She stretches her legs but she cannot touch the sandy bottom. Her arms are heavy, sodden as porous wood after a storm. She has lost her shoes. A sudden wave engulfs her, and for a moment Celia is tempted to relax and drop. Instead, she swims clumsily, steadily toward shore, sunk low like an overladen boat. Celia concentrates on the palms tossing their headdresses in the sky. Their messages jump from tree to tree with stolen electricity. No one but me, she thinks, is guarding the coast tonight.

Celia peels Jorge's letter from her housedress pocket and holds it in the air to dry. She walks back to the porch and waits for the fishermen, for daylight.

The Girl Typist Who Worked for a Provincial Ministry of Culture

María Eugenia Alegría Nuñez

THE PAGE FELL, and the typist never saw where. Completely mesmerized she goes about creating her inexhaustible world of words, between folding screens of paper and a thousand vegetable forms that creep along the colored mosaics, until they pile one version on top of the other in an inconceivable palimpsest of words never uttered but a thousand times heard that will become her work—enormous, endless, forged within the verbal wasteland that she is copying.

She shows the sun her solitude at midday. She drinks sweetened tea that sticks to the table, putting out incessant cigarettes. She had spent so many hours for so many years copying other people's writings that she began to mix her own words in with what she copied, and almost without wanting to or without thinking about it, a work of unexpected splendor was born. A work in which words spill over one another in battles where style decides the victory. Every transcript, every document or memo reaches its destination with unusual errata, words never before placed in that order, precise and brilliant like the rare light that makes them new, unexplored. Nobody knows where they come from, but everyone is thankful for that perfume in the midst of so much dryness.

One weary afternoon under the August sun, a bored and idle poet trapped in a girl typist's body began to collect all the tiresome pages with errata. When she collated them, she was surprised to discover a certain continuity. In obedience to a mysterious textual architecture, dazzling poems, stories, novels, and tales were composed, which were then trimmed down according to the flatness of what those lily white pages said, until only one novel emerged, rising up out of the union minutes, depositions, certificates, speeches, all that monotonous verbiage. It was an exceptional work, only comprehensible to initiates, those who not only knew the impenetrable lingo of official documents but also had the sensitivity to recognize interpolations. After years and years of typing so much verbal stupidity, the reading of the novel grew toward infinity. A new compilation and arrangement of all her office work during that period was necessary. The typist would put all that together carefully, with a few quick stylistic revisions, and from there her brilliant opus would emerge. It surged forth clean and beautiful, full of daring images that sprang from jumbled writings. Her first stories, her long poems that finally found their place in the composition of that one and only novel, created a narrative experience without precedent in the Spanish language. But the name of the author remained unknown. In spite of that notorious Cuban desire to honor individual accomplishments, plus the involvement of the secret services of the police and desperate attempts to track down the transcripts and documents that tumbled out from everywhere, authorship was never determined. Hundreds of girl typists put parts of their own lives and jobs into that tumultuous mass of paperwork circulating ceaselessly through the cultural bureaucracy.

The first interpreters of that body of literature tried hard to clear away what seemed to be pure rubbish. But when their work was practically finished, they doubted it had really been worthwhile. And feared that taking the typist's paragraphs and sentences out of the monotonous bureaucratic texts, was, in fact, some kind of terrible mutilation of that which had occasioned in the first place such a marvelous work. Because it was those very words of transcripts and documents, the endless repetition of the same expressions as in a bad popular song, that had given birth to the luminous ideas from which the typist's radiant poetry had sprung. She was definitely overwhelmed by the tedium but perhaps also bewitched by the rhythm of sentences repeated a thousand times, the same words empty of meaning, the wasted universe created by the colored mosaics, the folding screens of paper, familiar slogans, the incessant music of keys clicking in the office. Because we all know that the reproductive potential of words inundates everything. And when something is said or read or heard, it becomes real, takes on an existence of its own that rises above and finally imposes itself on our direct perception of things and people.

About that time, fierce literary discussions arose among critics until the problem was resolved into two schools, one of which demanded that the bureaucratic hogwash be expunged from the text like a diamond evolving out of carbon. That was called the Diamond School. The other school demanded textual integrity no matter how long the text turned out to be, which in some way vindicated the formality of bureaucratic lingo by recapturing its ritualistic function in society. That was the Ritual School. After many long and heated struggles in symposia, international conferences, and the academic press, the matter came to the attention of the international Spanish-speaking literary market, and several deluxe editions of the Diamond School were published that included the Complete Poetry, Stories, and Excerpts from the Novel with the impressive title of *A Light Shines in the Darkness*. On the other hand, the Ritual School broke all records worldwide with its publication of the Complete Works in sixty thousand volumes, where a select few could enjoy reading about everything that happened in official cultural circles in the Province of Matanzas from the 1970s to the 1990s. Finally all the typist's stories and poems, plus the long and marvelous novel, could be read in their entirety.

But the girl typist herself—sunk in a world of glasses of tea that stuck to tables, putting out incessant cigarettes, reading silly novelettes and watching soap operas—never knew of her anonymous fame, which spread all around the world to the glory of the word.

Translated by Lisa Davis

Zapata

Pablo Medina

MOSTLY WE DROVE through the swamp on our way to the Bay of Pigs, where the fishing was the best to be found anywhere on the island. The one road through went straight, with hardly a curve, into Playa Girón, which was to be the site of the ill-fated exile invasion in 1961. The sun was already setting when the first line was cast and it was only after the first light of dawn had tinted the eastern edge of the sky that we returned, laden with fish and ready to sleep through the morning.

From the car window, Zapata Swamp appeared as an endless expanse of brackish water and mangrove with an occasional *carbonero*'s shack. At times, columns of smoke in the distance rose toward the sky from, one imagined for they were never seen outright, slow burning coal ovens.

It happened that on a summer's day when I was eight years old and things were slow at the farm (the cane wasn't harvested until January), my mother's cousin Berto took a group of us crabbing in the swamp. We reached Zapata before dusk and stopped the jeep by a dirt road. To the right was a cow pasture; to the left, water as far as the eye could see—an inland shallow sea. Each of us, except my uncle Jaime, who carried a lantern, was handed a burlap sack and a hook fashioned out of a clothes hanger. The boys (myself and two cousins) were told to stay close to Jaime. As the sun went down, the crabs started creeping onto the road, at first only a few, then as it got darker, more and more came until the road was literally covered with them. They were ochre colored, about a foot long each, with claws as big as my hand, and they made eerie clacking and rasping noises as they crawled over each other. It was my first time crabbing and I was terrified, frozen in place by the morbid sensation that I could, at any time these creatures so wished, be devoured alive.

Everyone else was busy hooking the monsters by the large claw and dropping them into the sacks. This had to be done quickly, so as not to allow the crab to latch on to the hand holding the sack. "Those claws can really mangle a thumb," Berto had warned me with a cackle. Soon all the sacks but mine were filled and more were brought out. Jaime suggested we go into the cow pasture where we would find the females with their egg sacks bursting. To do this we had to crawl under a barbed-wire fence, the last strand of which lay dangerously close to the ground. Berto, his brother Raelo, Jaime, and my two cousins made it through easily, but as I slid under, I felt something hard under me. Thinking it was a crab (it was, most probably, a rock), I jerked up, slashing my back on one of the barbs. Within a minute or two my shirt was soaked with blood, and surrounding me was a cloud of mosquitoes as thick as coal smoke. I could barely see, I could barely breathe; I could not talk or even cry because I didn't want to swallow a mouthful of insects. My uncle took me back to the jeep, rolled up the windows, and told me to wait.

It was a hot night, as hot as it can get in the interior of Cuba. The inside of the jeep felt like a slow-burning oven. I was wet with my own blood; I was tired, alone, afraid, constantly watching the darkness outside, horrified that one of the *carboneros,* people who were said to practice the lowest of aberrations, from pederasty to infanticide, would show up. I waited in that metal coffin in such darkness I could not even see my hand in front of my face. I tried rolling the window down a crack to get some fresh air as the ferrous smell of my blood was making me nauseous, but within minutes a few mosquitoes had snuck in. Unable to see anything, I sat helplessly and listened to them buzzing round my ears until I could not bear it any longer. I leaned forward on the seat and waited for one of the little suckers to bite my bloody back. When I felt the prick, I threw myself backward hoping it would be too drunk with pleasure to escape. I don't know how many of the mosquitoes I crushed into oblivion; my strategy, however, kept me from going insane. It took me twenty years to recognize the value of that exercise. No matter how helpless the situation might really be, one's sense of helplessness will only be increased by inactivity. Few house fires will be put out with a garden hose, but the mere attempt will save one from the vise of despair.

The rest of the group showed up an eternity later with more crabs. The sacks were tied to the sides and top of the jeep, and we were ready for home. I felt the tension in every organ seep away in a long sigh of relief: bath, sleep, bath, sleep. But when Berto turned the key, nothing happened; the motor gave not even a whimper. The battery was dead. Now there were six of us inside the car sweating, cursing, and the crabs all around clacking and rasping.

Sometime after midnight we saw lights coming toward us in the distance. A truck full of soldiers with their Thompson machine guns and M-1's dangling limply over the sides pulled up next to us. A flashlight looked us over and fixed on Berto's face. He covered his eyes with his hand as if making a halfhearted salute. For a moment, there was absolute silence inside the cab—even the crabs stopped moving.

During the last years of the Batista dictatorship, groups of soldiers and police acting on their own (but with tacit official approval) roamed the interior in search of suspected sympathizers of the Revolution. Of these groups, the most notorious was one led by a man named Masferrer. They called themselves Los Tigres de Masferrer. I had heard stories of how they ripped open the wombs of pregnant women and tied naked men on the ground, close to a mound of red ants, after spreading molasses on their groins. I had seen Los Tigres photographed in *Bohemia,* a Cuban magazine, holding skulls of men and women they had supposedly tortured and killed. I was repulsed and, at the same time, fascinated by their sometimes ingenious methods. Their irrepressible brutality appealed to that part of me that sprinkled salt on toads and dropped live chameleons in jars of alcohol. This night, however, there was no fascination, only unadulterated trepidation.

Eventually, Berto got out and walked over to the truck's passenger seat. A low, barely audible murmur increased to loud talk and then open, if somewhat forced, laughter on Berto's part. A few minutes later he returned. "It's Captain Medeiros. He'll tow us to Jagüey." In the town the good captain woke up a mechanic who jump-started the jeep.

Berto gave the mechanic a sack of crabs. He did not give the captain anything, not then.

We arrived at La Luisa in the early morning hours and we found Mina waiting up. When she saw me, miserably dirty and pale, her face opened like the dawn that was just beginning to spread over the *ceibas* in the back of the house, and she smiled. She took off my shirt, washed and disinfected my back, and prepared some *café con leche* and a couple of slices of warm bread with homemade butter. That was the most delicious bread I have ever tasted.

Her Mother's House

Ana Menéndez

THE ROAD to her mother's house crossed a wooden bridge into a field of sugarcane that bent green and wide to the horizon before it narrowed into a path flanked on both sides by proud stands of royal palms. It was a late afternoon in summer and the men were coming in from the fields, hauling their machetes behind them. They stepped aside with their backs against the palms to let her pass and then stood waiting for the dust to settle, their hats flopping softly in the breeze. Lisette watched the men in the mirror until they retook the road and then her eyes were on the green fields ahead of her, the blue hills that dipped over the edge of sky. The thick warm air curled through the open window and the uneven road bumped her along in a seamless and predictable rhythm. She hummed a tune she had heard last night in the hotel and then she was silent, listening to the palm wind, the road beneath the wheels. It was the first time she had been alone in years and the new quiet seemed something she could touch, an opening in her chest that was as real as her childhood faith.

~

She was born in Miami, two years after the revolution. Her parents had met waiting in line at the Freedom Tower and married just two months later. He was a young student from Oriente, who'd come fleeing Batista. She was from a wealthy landowning family outside Varadero, who'd come fleeing Castro. For years, Lisette thought Batista Castro was one man, the all-powerful tyrant of the Caribbean, the bearded mulato who shot poor workers in the fields and stole her mother's house with all her photographs in it.

That house. Always in the air, behind every reproach. Her mother half mad with longing. And that winter morning when Lisette thought she began to know her mother. Twelve years old. Reading alone in her room, she heard the sobbing before she saw that her mother had crawled in on her knees, a long end of toilet paper in her hands.

"Look at this, feel how soft this is," she cried, holding out the paper to Lisette. "In Cuba today the little children have to use whatever scraps of paper they can find in the trash, bits of newspaper, cardboard. Oh, feel how soft this is."

Her mother had let her body drop to the floor and she lay there for a long time, shredding the paper into smaller and smaller pieces. Lisette sat at the edge of her bed, watching and waiting for her father to come in the room and gently lift her mother. She had turned to Lisette, her eyes open wide.

"When the soldiers came for the house, I walked straight, not turning once to look at the stained-glass windows," she cried softly now. "Not even the white columns that climbed to the second floor."

And the iron railing on the balcony where the rattan furniture was laid out for company, the clink of glasses. Lisette began to remember all of it too.

Lisette married a round-faced boy whose parents were from Varadero, a short drive from her mother's hometown. They each needed someone to agree with. After everything, she still kept the photo that made it into the society pages, Lisette smooth-faced and skinny in the billowy dress, Erminio's arm wrapped tight around her waist, as if already he worried she was a wisp of smoke, a thin memory of herself.

She was a new reporter, covering city hall and trying to find a world within the small concerns of small towns, the wider life in berms and set-asides. He was a young lawyer who hated the law and preferred to make poems out of her stories. Every Sunday, he recited his creations in a deep sleepy voice:

The
Sweetwater city council
today
approved preliminary plans for a new
shopping center on
the
corner
of
Eighth Street and 107th Avenue.

The first months, he waited for her to wake. He poured her the orange juice and the coffee and read her his newspaper poems. Some mornings, when the night's images had vanished, she would kiss him. And they would return to the bedroom and he would whisper her breath back to her.

Later, she began to linger in bed alone, waiting for him to go. Even after they stopped talking, he'd leave a poem by the toast. Paint a heart. Some mornings she could still smell him in the kitchen and her heart would turn.

At lunch she would take a sandwich and sit alone by the bay, imagining the stories in each ripple of water, each cloud that had the strength to push across the sky.

One Christmas Eve she sat apart from Erminio as she had for months and watched him with the women. He said something and they giggled, clapping their hands together like little girls playing at tea. How they loved him, his long frame and freckled skin. They sat in a circle around the pool, under the lights her father had strung from the second-floor balcony to the roof of the gazebo. It was one of those clear December nights that Lisette still loved about Miami, everything clean. One of her cousins produced a guitar and began to sing a bolero, a soft and sad contemplation behind the notes. The applause was slow. Her cousin's father took the guitar away. "Playing sad songs on Christmas, what kind of musician are you?" and he began to strum out an old danzón. Erminio stood and walked to where she was. He sat next to her, took her hand. He squeezed it. She looked at the pool, at the ripples of light.

"It makes me afraid," he said. "How much I need you."

Lisette moved her head with the music.

"It's true," he said. He squeezed her hand. She looked at him and he squeezed harder.

"You're hurting me," she said. "What's the matter with you?" She stood. The music stopped and the others looked up. Erminio sat staring down at the ground, his shoulders bent a little toward his chest. His right hand shook. "Can't you leave me alone for one minute?" Lisette whispered at him. "One minute."

It was terrible the way he kept believing that history would reignite the now. He really thought they could be like they were. Not just them. Everything. Everybody. It made Lisette want to scream. The past wasn't something you could play again like an old song.

Erminio got up and walked to the far end of the yard, falling away from the gazebo lights. Fine, go, she said. And already Lisette was regretting the night.

There were moments that seemed, in their first rush of happiness, strong enough to outrun the inevitable. The night in Isla Mujeres, the wet breeze and the call of fishermen. They had lain skin to skin, remembering, Lisette watching the reflected water draw patterns on the wall. Later, when he went down to phone his parents in Miami, she had wrapped herself in the blanket and slipped away to the terrace off the hallway to smoke a cigarette. She saw him return to their room. She watched him shut the door. She waited until the door flung open again and she saw Erminio pause in the hallway, his face gray. He turned toward the next room, as if listening. He passed his hand over his face and then made a sudden run for the stairs. She stepped out and called after him. He looked up and saw her. He ran back and swept her in the air. She cried. She wanted so badly to love him.

And then Lisette was in the back roads of Cuba thinking it had been so long since she'd been alone.

~

The green fields turned yellow and then brown. Lisette had set out from Havana in the early morning, but now the day was stiffening, the light falling in heavy sheets that made the loose gravel shimmer in the distance. She had been driving for more than five hours and the feeling began to creep on her that she had made a wrong turn somewhere.

But she drove on, the road desolate except for the royal palms that were so much like the stories she remembered. Her mother had shut her eyes when Lisette told her she was going to Cuba. It was a simple reporting trip, a stroke of luck. She wasn't going to explain to her mother things she could barely explain to herself. How every story needed a beginning. How her past had come to seem like a blank page, waiting for the truth to darken it.

Her mother had frowned. What kind of paper sends a young woman to Cuba alone, with the rafters churning more and more chaos. She had bent in closer and looked Lisette in the eyes. After a moment she had leaned back and put her hands in her lap. She wouldn't find the answers to her failures there, if that's what she thought. The remark had cut into Lisette. But she pretended not to understand. Maybe her mother could give her a map to the old house? Cuba's changed, it's not the Cuba I was born in, her mother had said. And then finally, It's a mistake for you to go now. The now was deliberate. And Lisette recognized it as part of the sentence her mother left unsaid: Now that you're divorced. Her mother had taken it hardest. Her family weren't failures. In the end, Lisette promised to go without the map or her mother's blessing. She knew the house was outside Varadero, near Cárdenas. She would find it on her own.

At the airport, her mother had parked and walked her to the terminal. Her face was puffy.

"So you're going."

Lisette nodded. Her mother hugged her and took her hand. She pressed a note.

In Havana, Lisette had worn her mother's map smooth, like tissue paper. The names had changed, but the streets remained. The Malecón still faced toward Miami even after all these years. On every old street, the billboards insisted on the revolution. "We defend the right to happiness" and "The revolution is eternal." Lisette thought back to her marriage. The reassurances built upon their own disintegration. The more they said I Love You, the more they knew it was an empty incantation. Still, she thought she had been right to come. The people had been kind. The police hadn't followed. In the mornings, when everything was fresh and new, she had thought that they had something here that her parents' generation had lost in exile. The feeling evaporated by the end of the day, replaced by a watery feeling that she would never understand herself, much less this country that seemed intent on killing itself slowly. And before she fell asleep each night, despair took her again.

The road curved and the fields were green again and the blue hills were visible to the south. A man approached on horseback, growing in relation to the hills with every step. She pulled to the side of the road and examined her mother's map. On the lower right-hand side, her mother had painted a large box and labeled it simply, M. Lisette looked outside at the expanse of palms and orange trees. Her mother and her cryptics. She was probably afraid Lisette would be stopped with an incriminating document. Lisette got out of the car and sat on the bumper to wait for the man. The afternoon was hot, but the air smelled of oranges as if it were dawn. Now and then a weak breeze moved through and made a sound in the grass. The man got closer, filling up more and more of the sky, until he was upon her and Lisette sat waving her soft map like a small flag.

The man took off his hat and nodded, as if unsure he would be understood. It had happened to her in Havana, and Lisette had been vaguely hurt that no one recognized her as Cuban.

"Buenas tardes," Lisette said, exaggerating the contours of the words so the man would have no doubt she was one of them.

He smiled. "¿En qué la puedo ayudar?"

Lisette showed him the map and pointed at the road that was supposed to lead to her mother's house. She pointed to the block in the right-hand corner, where the road branched to the right. She looked up.

"Militar," the man said and shrugged as if something struck him as silly. The notion of a military base in the middle of the campo? Her mother's precautions?

He took the map and studied it. Then he turned it upside down and nodded, smiling, to point where she was. If she continued this way past the small cane refinery and turned right on the first main road, she would pass the military installation on her right. Then if she took the first left, she should get to where she wanted to go. No photos at the military installation. He handed the map back. They'll take your camera.

Thank you, she said. "Gracias."

The man put his hat back on and watched her for a moment before returning to the road.

The military base looked deserted, but as she got closer, Lisette noticed one soldier standing in the middle of the road. She slowed. He was very young and held his rifle carelessly. She gripped the wheel as she came up beside him. Suddenly, he took a step out of the way. Lisette heard herself take a breath. The boy knocked his feet together and saluted. Lisette stared for a moment, then smiled. She thought of waving and decided instead to nod as she passed the boy. Surrounded now by the wet green of the countryside, Lisette doubted anyone had either the inclination or the money to follow anyone else. It was as if the whole country had agreed to stop caring. Only Miami still cared. And that made Lisette feel an unexpected pang for her parents. She took a left at the road the old man had told her to and began to rehearse what she would say to the people living there now. Apologies, of course: I can go away if you want. I only needed to see my mother's old room. Upstairs, near the back, the one with a balcony with an iron railing and a view of the rose garden.

If they let her, Lisette would take pictures for her father. Show him the lost space from where his wife had emerged, naked except for her stories. The first years of their marriage, all her mother did was talk about her lost plantation. Her father told Lisette how she used to lie in bed giving him imaginary tours of the house. The graceful stairway laced with gardenias in the summer, the marble fireplace her father had installed on a whim after visiting the States, the long white-shuttered windows that looked out over the gardens, the mar pacíficos, the royal palms. Your grandfather was the only one who could grow roses in Cuba. People came from as far as Oriente to see them.

Lisette turned onto the first opening in the field, a bumpy road of loose sand and stone. The men stepped aside to let her pass. The landscape was green and flat but for the hills. She came to the end of the road where it disappeared into a field of sugarcane. And in the next minute, Lisette was pressing her tongue to the roof of her mouth, determined not to cry, not now, not over something so stupid as the colors of afternoon. She got out and stood for a moment wondering if it wasn't too late to drive to Varadero. Get a room on the beach, come back in the morning.

She looked at the sky. It had cleared and the air seemed cooler by the cane. She got in the car and sat for a while. She was hungry and tired, not herself. She turned the car around and drove slowly back the way she'd come. When she came upon the field men, she drove beside them for a while until they got off the road to let her pass. But she stopped the car and rolled down the window. She didn't give them a chance to address her in English.

"Buenas tardes," she said.

The men looked at one another, then nodded.

She asked if they knew of the old Aruna house.

"Aruna?"

The men discussed it. The man she had addressed laid down his machete and came to her window. "Santo's grand-daughter?"

Lisette thought for a moment and then motioned to him to get closer as she stepped out of the car. She nodded. "Mabella's daughter."

The man's eyes narrowed before he turned to face the others.

"Oye, la hija de Mabi."

When he turned back to her, he was smiling. He took her hands. "I knew it, I knew it when I saw you, the same eyes."

"Lisidro Padron," he said, holding out his hand. "El carpintero. Your mother has told you about me probably?"

The other men crowded around her before she could disappoint Lisidro. Questions. Where were they? How were they? Any sisters? Are the old Arunas still alive? Lisette shook her head to the last one. Died in Venezuela a few years after the revolution. The man bent his head. He motioned back to his friends. "I'll take you to the house."

He paused and looked at Lisette, deciding something. "El viejo Matún and his wife are living there." Lisette shook her head like a question. "You don't know Matún and Alicia? They worked for your grandparents all their lives, since they were children almost. Matún was the only man who could grow roses in Cuba." Lisette raised her head and looked at Lisidro. After a moment she said, "Yes, of course, the roses."

Twice in the walk to the house, she tried to ask Lisidro something, a question about the winds this time of year, where the road emptied. But he walked on without turning, as if he hadn't heard her or thought her poorly bred for disturbing the silence this way. Their footsteps loosened the top thin layer of dirt on the road and sent up clouds of red-brown dust behind them. The royal palms had thinned and in between them, by the edge of the road, pink flowers grew, their petals curled under where they were beginning to brown. The air was still, the thin white clouds high in the sky, and Lisette thought again how much she often preferred the journey to the destination. Even when she was a girl and they made the long drives to visit her father's parents in Tampa, she had reveled in the passing trucks, the outposts of life, the burger joints and the dried-fruit stands, most of them gone now, the road long since widened. But those early mornings with the stars still out, she used to sit in the back and wish they would never get there, that their whole life could become this car trip. She felt it now, comfortable in her stride behind Lisidro, accustomed to the silence, not caring anymore where the road ended.

Lisidro stopped suddenly ahead of her. He turned back and waved his arm for her to hurry. He stood in front of a little iron gate painted white. He shouted into a tangle of trees and plants. Lisette came up beside him. A slender stone path led from the gate into the garden. Out of the foliage, as Lisette stood watching, came a short woman, bent over, her head covered in a black shawl. She came up to the gate, resting a brown hand on the latch, and looked into Lisette's eyes.

"La nieta de Aruna," Lisidro said. "Lisette, this is Alicia. She and Matún have been here. Have been taking care of things."

Alicia watched Lisette. Her eyes were dark brown, almost black. As Lisette watched, the woman's eyes filled with tears.

"Yes, I see the resemblance," she said.

Alicia's eyes shifted down and a tear fell slowly along her nose. Lisette put her hand over the woman's hand, like rough paper and dry as the road. Alicia turned to Lisidro and back again. She removed her hand from under Lisette's abruptly and wiped the corners of her eyes with the shawl.

"You are here to take the house."

The hardness of the woman's words startled Lisette. She looked from Lisidro to Alicia and brought her arms to her chest.

"I swear to you it's not that at all," Lisette said. "Never."

Lisidro put a hand on her shoulder and motioned with the other to go through the gate.

"La Señorita Aruna has no such intentions. She only wants to see the house. And then she'll leave."

Lisette nodded and looked back to Alicia, whose hand had come to rest on the latch again.

"The resemblance. It's quite striking," Alicia said. "Igualita."

Lisidro had to give her a small shove to get them through the gate.

When they came to the garden, the first thing Lisette saw was a rooster and then the dry dusty ground that it pecked and then a speckle of sunlight like a pebble and beyond it, above it, in a weak shadow, the house.

The house, the idea of her mother's house there in the shadow, is a present thought in this retelling, the way she described it to herself much later. Back then, standing next to Lisidro and Alicia, Lisette saw that it was a house, but it could not be the house she had come all this way to see. This was a house with small windows carved high on the uneven walls. A flat, pitted roof of red tile. A single front door, wooden and cracked. An iron latch that hung open. A house with small windows. Uneven walls. Red tiles. Iron latches. The house of someone else's imaginings, a different story. Beyond the house stood the blue hills and Cuba, green and unknown, the way the first Spaniards must have seen it before they brought their straight rows of cane, tamed the wild green with double stands of palms.

Lisette saw the way Lisidro bent his head toward this house, this little dream. His lips moved, wordless. Alicia took her hand. And then Lisette was sitting at a wood table inside a small kitchen. A kerosene stove, a bucket of oil, a yellowed basin filled with water, a refrigerator covered in silver tape, black at the edges. Lisidro kept moving his lips at Lisette. She blinked. Was that her laughter? Inside it was dark; the contrast with the outdoors made her eyes hurt. She tried to look at Alicia, her polished coconut face.

Then a small door from the back of the kitchen opened and in it stood a man, naked to the waist. He carried a black bucket of dimpled fruit. When he saw the stranger at the table, he put the bucket down. Lisidro moved his lips. The man threw his arms in the air. He picked Lisette out of the chair and hugged her.

He went back to the fruit and put the bucket on the table. He picked out two pieces and laid them on a sheet of newspaper. Lisette stared at the fruit. The man finally took one in his hand and split the skin with his fingernail. The fruit smelled like roses. Lisette hesitated. The others watched her. She bit, the taste gritty and sweet, nothing like the sticky red paste that was the only thing she had known of guava in Miami. She swallowed and looked up at the man. His lips moved. And the air came rushing back.

"Your mother tell you about the guava trees here?" he said, and Lisette hearing for the first time. "Biggest fruit in all of Cuba."

Matún sat down at the last chair and pulled it up close to Lisette.

"Oye, you okay?"

He turned to his wife.

"Oye, Alicia, tráele un baso de agua."

"No, no," Lisette said. "I don't need water. I'm okay."

"You're red. This heat."

"I'm okay. Thank you."

Lisette swallowed. Matún shook a guava at her slowly.

"Tu mamá," he began. Then shook his head. "I can't believe you're here. I always used to tell my wife, it's only a matter of time before Santo's people show up again. Ay. What a wonderful thing, eh?"

He stood and walked back to a small room. Alicia and Lisidro stayed behind at the table. Lisette closed her eyes to shut out the truth that sat with its arms crossed in front of her. And what of it! she wanted to shout. So she lied for years. So she lied! If only Lisette could get up now and return to the hotel in Havana, the men dancing on the Malecón, back to the Cuba she could talk about later, the simple stories of the rafters, the plain facts of their sadness.

"Are you comfortable?" Alicia asked.

Lisette opened her eyes and nodded. "Sí, gracias."

Matún returned with a small wooden picture frame. He handed it to Lisette. A little girl in pigtails sitting in that very kitchen, all the furniture the same, a bucket of guava in front of her.

"Tu mamá," Matún said. He shook his head, smiling.

"Your grandparents loved this house," Alicia said.

"We've tried to keep it up for them," Matún said. "Of course"—he waved his hands—"old age gets us all!" He laughed.

"Speaking of viejos—"

Lisidro stopped him. "Los viejos murieron en Venezuela."

"Ah. So sorry about your grandparents." Matún wiped his hands over his chest. "Now, you see, that makes me very sad to hear. They loved this house." Matún folded his hands. He was lost for a few seconds in contemplation. Lisidro cleared his throat. Were they waiting for Lisette to speak? She was afraid she might shout if she tried.

Matún sighed. "Of course, we didn't live here then. We lived out back." He pointed toward the window, past the empty yard. "It was a small house, ours was, nothing like this. I finally had to tear it down to build the chicken coop. You saw the roosters? Prize-winning. Back when they gave out prizes." Matún laughed again.

They were silent.

"Yes, your grandparents were very good people. There was never any problem because of"—he paused and rubbed his skin—"you know. Not with them. They'd make coffee here and holler out the back for us to come and sit with them. They had no problems that way." Alicia looked at him and then at her hands, folded on the table.

Lisette handed Matún the photograph.

"Same with us," Matún said, taking back the frame. "We'd make coffee, we'd call them over, we'd all sit together. We had no problems either. In some ways, it was better then." He looked at Lisidro and stopped. "We're just here taking care of the house. If you ever wanted to return—"

Lisette shook her head. "First time," she began. "What I mean is, if this is my first time here, how could I return?"

She looked around the table and thought to smile. Finally, Alicia laughed and they all joined in. Alicia took Lisette by the hand.

"Come, I'll show you the rest."

Lisette paused. She could see from where she sat that the rest was another small room with a chair and beyond that a room that she guessed to be where Matún and Alicia slept.

"No, gracias." Lisette pulled her hand out of Alicia's and patted her shoulder. "Later—I'll see it the next time."

"You can't come all this way and not see the house!" Matún shouted.

"It's okay," Alicia said, looking at Lisette. "She's tired."

"Yes, I'm enough tired from the trip."

"Nonsense!"

Matún took her by the hand.

"One minute only."

Lisette stood and nodded. She let her hand relax in Matún's.

The narrow hallway that ran from the kitchen connected a small sitting room to two back rooms, each painted green.

"Your mother slept here," Matún said with a flourish of his arm.

A lace curtain covered the top half of the window, darkening the room. A wooden dresser was pushed up against the corner, its knobs worn black and shiny. The narrow bed was straight and tidy under the window.

Matún followed her gaze and nodded.

"Everything here was hers."

The others walked out and Lisette stood for a moment at the door. She walked into the room, half hearing Matún, not seeing the small rug, the low double bed, the flowered curtain strung across one corner.

She turned and walked out, following a crack in the floorboards. Lisidro and Alicia sat in two rocking chairs. A broom leaned against the door.

"My mother—" Lisette began, then stopped. She turned toward the door. When she turned back, she could feel the heat in her cheeks.

"My husband would have been so pleased to see this," she said. "It's too bad." She folded her hands and said more to herself, "My husband, Erminio."

She let his name hang in the air. Alicia and Lisidro looked at one another, but no one spoke. Lisette breathed in and smiled. She took Matún's hands and kissed him on both cheeks.

"Gracias," she said. "I must go. I have much work."

Matún kissed her. Then he put his hands behind his back and turned his head to look out the small window as he spoke.

"You know. The government has been very helpful to us. Yes, very generous with us. They gave us this land when your grandparents left. Every Sunday, me and the wife drive the scooter to Havana and sell guavas and mangoes. We are not poor; we are doing very well," he said. "Thanks to our government and the grace of God."

Alicia pulled her shawl closer. The silence of the countryside was like a weight. Lisette looked from Alicia to Matún. He was nodding to himself. "Thanks to the grace of God."

Lisette reached into her purse as if she were looking for her map. Then she took Matún's hands. She pressed the bill.

"Un regalito," she whispered.

His eyes never changed expression until he closed them and bowed ever so slightly. Gratitude and reproach, the small space between knowing and forgetting.

~

Lisette walked through the hallways, dragging one piece of furniture after another. She didn't know what she was doing. She needed to do something. And so she moved the armchair into the family room, the bar stools out to the pool. She stood and remembered the lights her father had strung all those years ago, that Christmas when the women loved Erminio. The gazebo was shabby now, a vein of mold running down one column. The lawn had grown over the flowers. It was as if the house had declined in sympathy with her father. In the last days of his illness, the Coral Gables code-enforcement board had sent them a complaint about the tall grass. Lisette had run two red lights in her anger. At city hall, she had ranted about the rights of man until a security guard escorted her out. She had regretted it and written a letter of apology later, a very proper repentance. She was an editor at the paper now, had her own office overlooking the bay. She was a little in love with a German psychologist who loved her back. In the evenings they had long conversations about the will and happiness. On Sundays, they had some people from his practice for lunch and she put out her good crystal and the leather-bound Rilke.

When, alone with him, the people gone home, she would complain of despair, her sick parents, he would hold her face and tenderly ask, "Why do you not kill yourself?"

It was an old joke with them. And Lisette always laughed. Logotherapy, he called it the first time. And she'd understood loco therapy. There is meaning in this, he insisted. And he waved his arms, meaning everything. Yes, she'd said, it's all loco.

Lisette stopped at the door to her old room. She walked to the closet. From the top shelf she pulled down a box and sat on the bed. It was the kind of box young women keep, and she hadn't opened it since her last weeks in college. A graduation program sat on the top, yellowed and brittle and almost twenty years old. Bits of the foil that condoms came wrapped in. A dried corsage from her junior prom. A translucent pink cocktail stirrer whose origins had long ago disappeared into her memory. Below, near the bottom, a pink diary with a lock and a stack of photographs tight in a rubber band. Lisette winced. Had this been her life?

She sifted through the letters, names she'd forgotten, dates and places. She stopped, reached to her chest for her glasses. Love letters. Letters from friends. One note on linen paper, which she opened, the paper crackling back into the present.

L.:

So happy you've finally decided to write that novel. I
think the Cuban experience is a great idea for a
book. You have to promise me one thing: You have
to make fun of them. There's no other way to write
this. Send me what you have.

Love you. Miss you. Can't wait to see you.

A.

The letter was typed, as if the sender wanted to remove
the last trace of himself. She couldn't remember receiving
it. Who was A.? Had she ever thought of writing a novel?
She remembered writers she'd known in college, students,
a man who had followed her for days. Was it the editor who
had told her she had Great Potential? A lover? A prankster?
Her ex-husband?

Had she written the note herself? She sat at her old bed
and tried to reach back into the years. She met herself going
the other way. Promising she would never write, never publish, never be a special section in the bookstore. Better to
write about berms and set-asides, last night's vote in a small
room of microphones and lights.

She took a pencil from the box. She read the letter again
and folded it in half. She stared for a moment at her hand.
And then she began to write:

Beautiful Coral Gables home, five bedrooms, three
baths, vaulted ceilings in the dining room. Balcony
with wrought-iron railings overlooking large pool.
Entrance flanked by royal palms.

She paused and added,

The house of your dreams.

Outside by the gazebo, she slipped the letter into her pocket. She stood still to hear a peacock send its melancholy wail through the yard. A car passed the house slowly, its engine low and hungry. Tomorrow she would air the house out and the next day she would call the realtor, tell her she was in a hurry. She walked up the creaking wood steps and sat on the railing, looking out over the fraying yard. Her parents had thrown a party here after she'd returned from Cuba, all of them healthy and young, the orange trees in blossom, her cousin's daughters splashing in the pool. She'd looked up at the house, the palms framed against the sky.

What was it like? What was the house like? The children's laughter like punctuation marks.

Only her mother was silent. She sat across from her, her hands in her lap. Lisette followed her gaze. The day was bright, shimmering above the water. Lisette spoke slowly. It was too bad, she began, that the soldier had taken her camera. There was so much to see. The road to the house that crossed a wooden bridge into a field of sugarcane. The narrow path flanked on both sides by royal palms. It was a late afternoon in summer and the men were coming in from the fields, their hats flopping softly in the breeze.

But the house. What about the house?

Lisette paused, making a circle with her arms. She looked at her mother. Watched her hands turn in her lap.

"Everything was the same," Lisette said after a moment. "The stairway, the balconies. Even the marble fireplace. Somehow, it all made it through the revolution."

She faced her mother. Held her chin in her hands.

"And the long white-shuttered windows that looked over the rose garden still let in the very brightest sunshine."

The children had stopped by the edge of the pool to listen. One by one they moved away to resume their game. Her father let his gaze fall. Lisette's mother looked up. She stood and Lisette watched her go. Her cousin came out with the guitar. The chatter of the afternoon resumed. Someone passed by and patted her on the head.

Lisette closed her eyes. The guitar played a slow bolero and Lisette remembered Erminio, his Sunday poems; she saw him again against the light, pouring her morning coffee. He had wrapped his arms around her tight, held her steady against the day.

Don Cayetano, the Unreliable

Alfonso Hernández Catá

DON CAYETANO left his house on Jesús del Monte every morning at eight thirty, a little blue cloud of cigar smoke trailing behind him, and walked with half steps to the trolley line. To those who passed him, it was as if they were seeing an antique engraving come to life.

He was tall and well proportioned; his wrinkled face was framed and studded with the white silver of his hair, sideburns, and luxuriant mustache that made the lively blackness of his eyes shine. Wearing a nearly impeccable white suit, a Panama hat that looked like undulating marble, and flashing a gold tooth that lent gravity to his childlike smile, he looked like someone waiting for a horse-drawn cab or an open carriage rather than an electric vehicle.

He epitomized the fundamental characteristics of the Creole. His unpretentious grace and aristocratic simplicity brought both Spanish nobility and Cuban good will simultaneously to mind in a single image. He could as easily be imagined holding his right hand over his heart between a lace collar and the gold pommel of a sword as wearing a *guayabera* decorated with five-pointed stars, carrying a machete, and sporting a wide-brimmed hat worn back on his head, the better to show his joyous face beneath the cockade.

"That boy knows the flavors of guanábana and the rhythms of *son* ringing through a shack, but he also knows the good life of the Iberian Peninsula," proudly declared the nearly hundred-year-old Black woman, formerly the family's house slave, who would always consider don Cayetano to be something of a child.

He was so satisfied with this fortunate combination of races and with his Basque surname, Arrechavaleta, that he was equally proud of only one other thing: his reliability. He inherited it from his father, who was ruined in the Ten Years War of 1868–78 and retired to Spain. "Swallow three times before giving your word, but spit your life out of your mouth three times before breaking it," he used to tell him. His dedication to backing up his promise with his whole soul made him prudent and trustworthy, qualities that allowed him to make his fortune once again.

His reliability became legendary: "A promise from don Cayetano is as good as having it in your hand," said some; and others: "Arrechavaleta's word is a done deed." He never proceeded to a second clause without clarifying irrevocably the previous one, and once an agreement had been reached and he had given his yes or no, he would hold out his right hand, tracing in the air an invisible flourish that was already present in his eyes. This gesture was his signature, his "I do solemnly swear."

This virtue came to be so extreme that it skirted the borders of vice. "Scraps of paper, judgments, and scribes are for swindlers," he declared. And because he lived off speculation and contributed to the earth's rich abundance, the wisdom of the countryside, and all the talents of the colonists, his pastures flourished and his sugar mills were mechanized without anyone casting an envious an envious or dissatisfied shadow over his prosperity.

The harsh harbingers of the patriotic eruption of 1895 put him to the test. As the son of a Spaniard, he strove always to remain equidistant between the two diametrically opposed passions while maintaining such evident dignity that he would never be suspected of pandering to either side. He had married a Cuban woman and he was Cuban, and his two sons were Cuban; but far away, in the northern mists of the Bay of Biscay, an old man awaiting death would have shed a bitter tear in his final hour if his youngest son— the other two were in Argentina and Chile: prodigal seed of the Spanish adventurer—had raised arms against Spain.

It was a painful dilemma, so clearly painful that no one ever suspected that it was the comforts of home or fear of the perils in the jungle that held him back. But his abstention was not enough: the times were struck by passionate lightning, no longer deeds, no longer words: even silence was open to interpretation and leaving became unavoidable. But where could he go? Spain? No. He would have found the same storm but on the opposite shore, and more to the point, he would still have the same problem.

The family moved to Tampa and from there, watched the first offensives of the revolution. The boys grew older, and their souls expressed themselves in words. Don Cayetano didn't dare curb their patriotic voices, which were like the voice of his own mute soul. One day, on his way to pick them up he came upon a public meeting where a man with a broad forehead, visionary eyes, and a manner of speaking as metallic as it was silken, conjured up for the crowd the still nonexistent image of an independent Cuba.

As he was leaving, after the enthusiastic cheers, a group of people congregated around the orator. Don Cayetano, unable to separate himself from the crowd, remained with them, thirstily drinking in the words that acquired an even more persuasive eloquence at close range.

"He who is not free to give his life to the cause should give something of his property, his ideas, or his sympathy . . . If money were not absolutely necessary, we would ask only for hearts and souls. The struggle, when it is fair, when it is just, needs smiles as much as it needs blood. It must make the intellectual virtuous and the indifferent useful."

Don Cayetano felt that these phrases were meant for him. It must have been the anointed voice of this preacher of destruction that made his words seem humanitarian, reasonable, essential, and tender. To form militias, undoubtedly the imperative tone of Ignatius of Loyola, his ancestral saint, would be more effective than this soft lilt that imbued the words with flowers—little red flowers, stained with blood that could be washed off later. But he, who probably would not have followed the severe saint, docilely followed the sounds of this seraphic voice.

Later, much later, he managed to be alone with the captivator of souls, and he said to him:

"I am not free to go to war: but I want to contribute to it . . . If some day, God willing, I find myself free, I will go . . . I will go, on my word! Tomorrow I will send you three thousand pesos."

"Thank you in the name of Cuba. I will send you a provisional receipt as soon as possible."

"No, no . . . no paper. I don't give my word in writing, and I want nothing in writing in return. Three thousand pesos. Done!"

And he held up his right hand to trace his flourish in the air.

A smile lit up the noble face with the broad forehead and luminous eyes, and his voice grew merry while he clapped his hands:

"Now I know who you are! Don Cayetano Arrechavaleta . . . Allow me to press to my heart your honorable chest. I have heard so much about you that I feel as if I know you. No, don't interrupt me . . . Happy is he who succeeds in making a legend of his integrity."

By the time don Cayetano received a letter of condolence from Spain on the death of his father and could go about keeping his promise to go to war, the heroic remains of many already lay in the fields and fresh vigor spilled out from the horizon, still pregnant with night.

It was only six months of hope and fatigue. But during that time he knew weariness, a hammock swinging between two trees, the sudden sounds of gunshots, rugged rides on horseback, warnings, gunfire, thirst, unbandaged wounds, the treachery of fear and of some men, brief respites in the homes of prefects, boiled corn and green mangoes. And when the blessed hour arrived to enter Havana with the Generalísimo, even those who had been in the jungle from the beginning couldn't help but treat him as one of them.

After the thrill of the first taste of freedom diminished, don Cayetano preferred not to stay on the tumultuous and already barren path of the struggle: he hung up his machete and his cartridge belt, left behind the conflicts in the city,

and went off to rebuild his *finca* that had been ruined yet
again. Only his integrity and reliability could win out over
those who would take advantage of the chaos. He mapped
out boundaries, hired workers, plowed, tilled, and sowed.
And his was the first crop harvested on free land. One year
later, the green sea of sugar fields undulated in the breeze.
. . . A year later and not before: even in the most benevolent land in the world, the plow is slower than the sword.

Don Cayetano was content. . . . The price of sugar went
up and up. Every month it was a quarter of a centavo more,
and day after day greed drove the Wall Street vampire to
buy more sugar mills. And, if the agent wasn't fooling
him—and since he was his agent, he was the most reliable
of all—he was about to make a marvelous business deal!
Given that his last two sugar cane harvests had brought in
a hundred thousand bags, the representatives of the Yankee
trust could very well offer that enormous sum. He was
going to be rich, very rich, without a care, without owing
the banks! Rich enough to be able to relax and take a long
trip; rich like don Nicolás Castanos; rich enough not to
worry that his sons, Bebito and Tano, gambled hard at the
Union Club and owned three motor vehicles, while he took
the trolley. He was going to be rich! That night he would
meet with his agent and the two Americans in the Paris
Restaurant, and the following morning, even though for
him it wouldn't have been necessary, they would go to the
solicitor's office to draft the document. . . . He was going to
be rich!

The meeting was brief but tiresome. Contrary to their
expectations, don Cayetano and his agent were not the ones
to push the deal. In slow and nasal voices, the Americans

hammered away: "Be it understood that tomorrow morning at nine o'clock . . . at nine o'clock, so that we can catch
the boat . . . City Bank will guarantee the deal . . . If the
gentleman wants an advance, or we can at least sign an
option . . ."

Don Cayetano grew angry. Wasn't his word worth more
than all the advances and options in the world? As the saying goes, a scoundrel can escape through the center of the
"o" of an "or." He had given his word, and nothing more was
needed. The agent must have explained in English about
don Cayetano's reputation and renown, because the Anglo
Saxons stood up and apologized profusely, regarding him
with semi shocked curiosity, without daring to say that in
the sea of business, reliability was a shipwreck. And still, on
taking their leave, they again repeated:

"We are delighted that you are such a gentleman . . .
Tomorrow at nine, then, at the solicitor's."

Don Cayetano returned home somewhat agitated. What
could it be? Too much to eat? The effort of following a broken conversation? He felt burdened. He couldn't read the
supplement of *El Diario*, as was his habit. He opened the
window and eventually the scent of jasmine and heliotrope
disturbed him. . . . Fearing insomnia, he took the precau-
tion—almost never necessary—of setting the alarm clock
for seven. Despite his fears, he fell asleep quickly, but he
didn't sleep as he usually did: it was as if he remained deli-
cately balanced on that thin line between wakefulness and
sleep.

His nose could distinguish between the scents of the
different fruits and flowers from the patio; he saw the window, the flaming bright leaves of the *flamboyan* tree, the

calm moon that turned the white limestone walls to gray. After experiencing even more intense uneasiness, he saw the door open little by little, and toward him walked a man cloaked in mysterious shadows through which only his eyes and forehead could be discerned.

He wanted to jump up and grab a weapon, but he couldn't. A soothing gesture gently allayed his anxiety. And a voice, also calming, began to speak to him in soft reproach. Where had he heard that voice before?

And the voice said:

"What are you going to do, don Cayetano, Cuban son of a Basque father and a Cuban mother, what are you going to do? Your word is your pride, and you have given it; but you have given it for something that is not entirely yours. You are going to sell your plantation. You are going to exchange it for a mountain of gold—gold with no roots, gold that can come and go anywhere—the fertile plains and glens, the valley of Yumurí, and that spot where a palm grove casts shadows on the ground like stars falling from branches; soothing shade where children always take refuge . . . You have given your word. But you don't know that it's been said: 'The tongue has sworn but the heart has not.' Your lips gave your word, but only after your conscience had hardened. It would be better, and you know it, to say with dignity, 'I made a mistake,' than to keep a ridiculous promise, above all, an unjust and immoral promise, which is punishable by another Code that is stricter than the one courts and lawyers follow. I'm not exaggerating. I would be more likely to do the opposite, out of respect for you. Let's see: Could you promise to sell your name? Arrechavaleta belongs to your parents and your children.

You have it on loan. It's the same with the land. The land belongs to the grandparents and the children. It's fertilized with the bones of our compatriots, watered with blood and tears. While you were fighting in Las Villas, other Cubans were fighting all over Cuba, on your plantation as well. Because we are few and we have struggled so much, there is scarcely any land from San Antonio to Maisí where the dead have not fallen. The mists that cover your ranch at twilight are the dreams of a hundred generations. If you retreat to your mountain of gold, you will find nothing. If you retreat to your plains, your valley, your glens filled in the afternoons with violet-colored shadows, you will find the glistening waters of our Caribbean Sea . . . It's not enough that you have made of our land a diabetic country at the mercy of neighboring markets; now you want to market the land itself, the sacred land whose sale will be thrown back at you by everyone from Hatuey to the last descendant of the last fertile Cuban womb. No, don't contaminate your heart with the gold of that tooth that glitters between your lips! No, Cayetano Arrechavaleta, not you, not you! You fought for freedom; one must fight for freedom every minute in a thousand ways, and now you are a soldier in the vanguard of the decisive battle. War never begins with the first battle nor ends with the last . . . Now we must reorganize, consolidate, fight against the worst parts of our very selves—vanity and anger—which are always exacerbated after the fight. I know that you have pledged your word, made your promise; nevertheless, today your must erase that flourish your hand made in the air. For once, don't be reliable—yes, it's a great sacrifice! But weigh in the balance what we all hold in our conscience; put money to one side and to the other, the scents that surround you, the air that envelopes you, the bed in a free land that will one day replace, forever, that bed where you now lie . . . No, you will not sell the small piece of the homeland that is yours, almost yours! Cayetano Arrechavaleta, you will not sell . . . Is it true that you will not sell?"

An anguished shudder ran through his reclining body. Once again, he wanted to move toward the apparition and his mouth spoke without the need of words.

"Who are you to speak to me in this manner? Where have I heard your voice before? Why does your voice move me so deeply and send new emotions through my being? Tell me your name . . . Who are you? Who are you?"

The shadow smiled softly and spoke these four luminous words in a whisper:

"I am José Martí."

As the alarm clock vibrated, a blanket fell in repeated folds over him until it drowned out the chiming. With his eyelids shut tight, welcoming a sleep full of gaps open to reality, don Cayetano slept until very late. The telephone calls from the solicitor and the three visits from the agent were all in vain. Faithful to his instructions, the servant told everyone who came to look for him that he had left for the countryside.

News of the first instance of his unreliability was commented upon in that awestruck tone in which one speaks of phenomena that violate the great laws of nature. And with the relentless injustice that demands everything of someone who has already given almost everything, it took only a few hours for a shadow to be cast over his many years of impeccable living. "What do you think about what

Arrechavaleta did?" "You can't trust anyone." "Maybe he wanted even more money." "No, that's impossible." The most expert financiers were sure that a bad deal had been made. But every time some tactless person mentioned his incomprehensible behavior, don Cayetano said:

"Please call me don Cayetano the unreliable. Yes, I deserve it. I made a promise and I broke it. I gave my word and did not follow through."

And he offered a contented smile, as if underneath his self-reproach, in the depths of his soul, he coveted an ineffable secret.

Translated by Barbara Paschke

Not the Truth, Not a Lie

Uva de Aragón

BURSTING WITH JOY, José María walked across the sand at dawn, leaping lightly with a happy step. Sometimes he stopped and his hungry, dreamy eyes caressed the landscape. He would then feel calm and allow the beauty surrounding him to penetrate his eyes and each one of his pores. He felt breeze, sea, and skin as a single entity, solid and inseparable.

Later, people would come. There would be noise. But at this early hour, the beach was his, his alone. The boy experienced the sensual pleasure of possession.

He stretched out on the white sand. Spread his dark arms. From above, he looked like Christ . . . or a cross.

Then he rose. He ran to the water's edge. Foam kissed his feet, because the sea loved him. Facing the sea, José María was huge and endless, like the waters.

The sea. The sea? The boy wondered whether the sea was male or female because for him it possessed human attributes. José María spoke to it as if it were a man. He talked about his plans, his dreams, and his concerns. Sometimes, when he felt anger eating up his insides, the sea shared his rage. He heard it also roar with fury. He heard it curse. How manly José María's sea was then!

But at other times, the sea was like a mother, lulling him and rocking him tenderly on her lap, caressing him with her breath, suckling him, giving him life from her own life.

At night the sea sometimes frightened him. He felt the dark immensity was like a woman who is both feared and desired. He hears seductive voices tempting him. As if a magnet were attracting him with a tireless force. What might await him in the distant depths of the waters?

José María loved the sea most of all at sunrise, when the tenuous clarity of dawn softened the shapes of things. Sometimes he believed the waves would carry him to a far-away beach—he didn't know if this was a memory or an omen—where there would be no fear, no worry, no broken dreams.

"You can't imagine how many mornings, José María, I watched you from my bedroom during your daily communion with the sea. Although the sea belongs to everyone, for me, José María . . . it's a bit more yours than anyone else's.

"That summer, do you remember?"

"How could I forget!" you respond.

"We were on vacation. Well, I was on vacation. You were living there. Living? What does living mean for a poor boy, a poor black child? Did you know, José María, that I envied you? No . . . don't laugh. To me you were free . . ."

"Free?"

"What sarcasm I hear in your voice! Your ironic tone is so piercing. Be quiet. Be quiet, Josemaía.

If you only knew . . . I saw you running at dawn. More than once I had to rub my eyes, because I thought I saw you with wings. I thought you were so smart, because you could read the movement of the stars. You could tell time by the sun. You knew the names of plants, where the crabs hid, and how to catch them. The pure sciences were so easy for you; for me they were forbidden.

I, on the other hand, felt imprisoned by my fine organza dresses and my schoolbooks, sitting in classrooms listening to professors whose hair and minds time had turned gray. Such strong bars confined me in my ivory tower. My world without horizons was a glass case where the polluted air pushed against the walls, forming huge whirlwinds in its search for freedom.

How I would have preferred to go barefoot like you instead of wearing those imported patent leather shoes. Your worn out clothes looked much more beautiful to me than my blouses of silk and French lace. Penniless? Yes, you were penniless. You were you. And I, who was I under those clothes that bound me?

But I was a prisoner, you tell me. A prisoner of my dark skin, of my birth, of my poverty. Of my own hatred. Of my envy and jealousy. Of my dreams.

"Do you remember the first time we saw each other?"

"You were dressed in white."

"Then you remember, Josemaía?"

"Yes. And I even remember what I thought when I saw you. Or rather, what I felt. I felt even darker!"

"I pretended to want to help you, but really, I did it more for myself than for you. But your mother—poor Cacha— with her old wooden slippers and her smile—as sad and tired as her step—announced so proudly:

"The señorita is going to teach Josemaía to read . . ."

You seemed even taller and stronger to your mother as soon as you began to read. You learned very quickly. Too quickly I thought, and I felt a strange kind of sadness.

Reading. A new world with infinite horizons. The world is yours, Josemaía. The past. The future. Conquer them! Run! You're free. Fly with those wings that dawn drapes over your dark shoulders.

But the present? The present is not yours, Josemaía. I don't know to whom it belongs. The wealthy? The politicians? The military? The Church?

We became friends. You laugh? You rascal! Have you forgotten? I gave you my most prized possession. That book, written by that good man, the one with the broad forehead and eyes radiant and deep like the dreams of all humanity. The book with the poem about the princes and the tale of the three heroes. You were my only prince and hero, Josemaía.

You taught me the names of the stars. I even learned how to catch crabs, those nights we escaped to the wharf!

I was free that summer. You taught me to be free. I buried my patent leather shoes in the sand. I bared my feet. And my soul, too . . . a little.

Your eyes look doubtful . . ."

"Yes, because I was black!"

"What a bitter response! But I loved you. Why don't you believe me? Tell me, why . . . ?"

"Why did I do it?"

"When they told me—if only you knew how I suffered! I had never cried so much. Why are you laughing, José?"

"You weren't crying for me. You were crying for your broken toy. You went back to the city. To your classrooms and your laces, as you say. You knew that I'd been caught stealing, that I'd gone to prison. And you cried?"

"Don't talk that way, Josemaía. You're hurting me."

"I'm hurting you! And what did you do to me? Don't you see that you let me taste the honey and then you took the honeycomb away with you? Don't you know that you planted in me the longing to learn, when I was condemned to live with no other text than my poverty? You snatched away the world you opened up to me. The beach was so lonely without you! It was summer and it seemed like January. I felt cold the first night you were gone."

"But my mother was making inquiries about getting you a scholarship . . . I had promised you . . ."

"My dear, my dear girl dressed in white, I was born without hope. I didn't believe in anyone."

"And then what happened?"

"You know . . . Years went by . . . the Revolution came."

"And you believed in it. They told me you believed in it."

"And they also told you that I went to your house, that the mob came with me and attacked and looted the place. I was in the lead. Don't cry. No, it's not a lie, but it's not the truth either. Do you know that everything is like that, not the truth, not a lie? Yes, I was there. Yes, everything happened just like they said. But . . . I went there looking for you and you weren't there! I fled . . . I ran . . ."

"No, Josemaía, you flew . . . because you have wings."

"Then I flew, if you say so."

"That's when it happened?"

While seeking asylum in a foreign embassy, a general of the defeated army met with forces of the rebel militia. Their commander declared that the death of the general's daughter had been an accident.

"Yes, it was then, while I was running, that I saw you. The bullet pierced your chest. Blood burst out over your white clothes. It looked as if your heart had left your body . . ."

"Finally I was free, Josemaía, free!"

"But I was still a prisoner. And I kept running . . . or flying."

"I know where you went. To the sea, right?"

"Yes, and when I got there, it was night."

While fulfilling his duty, a young member of the Rebel Army died on the beach, defending with his very life the Revolution that had freed him from oppression and poverty. José María Valdés drowned. Exhausted from long hours on guard duty, he apparently fell asleep and was swept away by the incoming tide.

"But it wasn't like that, was it, Josemaía?"

"No. I wasn't asleep. I walked into the tide. I walked into the waves that were calling me. I felt a voice. I heard my name spoken more beautifully than I had ever heard it before.

JOSEMAÍA . . . Josemaíaa . . . Josemaaíaaa . . .

It was a whisper and it was an order. It was the end it was the beginning. Death and life. It was you. And it was me."

It's a strange legend, to be sure. But I thought I saw two children on the beach: a black boy, sparsely clothed, and a young girl, dressed in white. They were running hand-in-hand toward the rising sun, bursting with such joy that they couldn't be ghosts. Anyway, I don't believe in such things.

Translated by Barbara Paschke

Old Rosa

Reinaldo Arenas

IN THE END she went out to the yard, almost enveloped in flames, leaned against the tamarind tree that no longer flowered, and began to cry in such a way that the tears seemed never to have begun, but to have been there always, flooding her eyes, producing that creaking noise, like the noise of the house at the moment when the flames made the strongest posts totter and the flashing frame came down in an enormous crackling that pierced the night like a volley of fireworks. She went on crying, and her face, shrouded in a reddish halo, looked at times like the face of a little girl lost in the middle of one of those storms that only occur in hallucinatory illustrations accompanying stories of witches and other phantasmagorias, which she had never read. But now and then, when the flames exploded almost before her eyes, singeing her lashes, her face lit up with all the features that time had undertaken to etch there. Then it could be seen, clearly, that this was an old woman. And had one of the neighbors passed by, he would have confirmed that this woman could be none other than Old Rosa. The brands, still flaming, were leaping into the air and tumbling down over the towering weeds in the yard. The fire was feeding upon itself, rising up all around in a sudden surge and threatening to strike the woman, making her breathing more difficult every moment. She was surrounded by the flames, and had she screamed, it is possible that no one would have heard her cry, indistinguishable in the snapping of the weeds and the explosion of the trees, which were even then dissolving in the air, transformed into evanescent swirls of ash. She was surrounded by fire, and in other times, terrified, she might have said, or at least might have imagined: *My God, this is hell.* And even if she had felt lost she might have started to pray. But now she was not praying, not calling out, not even seeing the fire that was already leaping impatiently up to her skirt. She was seeing, and this is true, other realities even more important to her. At her side there were not flames, not weeds, not crackling, not even the smoldering ruins of the house; and she was only Rosa, for it would not have occurred to anyone to attach to this remarkably young woman (with those terrific legs she had mysteriously preserved without a scratch) the epithet *old*. She was only Rosa. Rosa, Tano's daughter; Rosa, the little one in the family; Rosa, the one who had actually listened to transistor radios; Rosa, the one with the perfect legs. Rosa, Pablo's woman. And Pablo arrived, as he did every Sunday, and headed toward the house, jingling his spurs, whistling, ambling with his young colt's gait that was far more graceful than the gait of the horse he rode away on every afternoon, after having chatted for a moment with the old man, after having grasped her hands in his and asked her to let him sit on the sofa, next to her, for the wedding would be very soon. But she, as always, not only forbade him to sit at her side, she also withdrew her hand and recited the words *honor,* and *family,* and *respect.* And Pablo moved uneasily in his chair, and when it came time to leave he stood up very solemnly, with his hands in his pockets. And now, the explosion of the last uprights supporting the house merged with the explosion of the chicken coops and the custard apple tree, and a flock of screeching birds fell singed before her unseeing eyes. The tamarind tree glowed red, and the lowest branches crackled softly at the touch of the first flames. It was the day of the wedding, and she went, as always, to give the hens their corn, and she felt for those who were ready to lay, and with a stone she killed a rat that was eating the newborn chicks; then she went to the well, drew a bucket of cold water, and washed herself in the bathhouse, behind the shed for the calabashes and the corn. The guests were arriving, and she greeted them all, and offered them coconut nougats and a punch that was quite watery, almost a lemonade. And the house was filling up with people, until even the Pupo sisters were there. *Those miserable whores,* she thought. And she became furious. And she ordered her mother to throw them out of the house or there would be no wedding. But just then Pablo arrived from the mango grove; he had tied the horse up and was already in the breezeway. The bridegroom entered, and pandemonium broke out among the guests; the youngest ones ran to greet him, and patted him on the back, and spoke to him, smiling, whispering in his ears. How lucky you are, one of the Pupo girls dared to say to her, maliciously, looking toward Pablo. But she did not answer; she averted her eyes, turned her back, and went to the kitchen, where her mother and other old women from the countryside were preparing the meal and the sweets. There aren't going to be enough coconut nougats, she said. Shortly afterward an automobile could be seen coming down over the plain. All the boys went out onto the porch. Here comes the priest, they shouted. And they ran up to the fence, and solemnly watched how that prominent man, dressed in a black frock and sandals, got out of the car, greeted them, and started to walk toward the house. The priest entered the living room, and everyone stood up; some of the men crossed themselves, and the women carried their little ones to him so he could bless them. The priest ascertained how many children had not been baptized and proposed a collective baptism for the following week. Then the wedding began. Rosa saw herself surrounded by the lights of tall candles glittering between the areca palms that her mother had arranged on the makeshift altar; she looked at Pablo, who was now watching very solemnly as the priest gave the benediction with a raised hand; beyond him she noted the bowed heads of the guests, the boys perched in the windows, the tearful old women blowing their noses in the corners, the Pupo girls, sad, watching her from the middle of the room, where the afternoon glow spilled in through the doorway and flooded over them, giving them a look of complete desolation. Then she stared at them fixedly, as if challenging them, and smiled to herself. At midnight the two of them, she and Pablo, left the house; he in front, on the horse's saddle; she on the rump, holding fast to the man's waist. The horse bucked, Pablo spurred it; and the three of them disappeared over the plain. Later they picked up the main road. When they came to a grove of trees beside a brook, Pablo reined in the horse, jumped down, took her by the waist, and seated her in the tall grass. I can't

hold out till we get to the house, he said. We're going to stop
here, and afterward we'll go on. Rosa, we're married now,
he continued. And he was breathing heavily. And his voice
came out very hoarse and low. She, still dazed by the wild
horseback ride, did not know what to say. There's still a very
long way to go, he said, and he pulled her to him. And she
felt something like another powerful arm rubbing against
her thighs. And suddenly she threw the man off, looked at
him, almost terrified, slapped him across the face, and took
off running toward the horse, which was impassively eating
daisies by the brook. Very solemnly, they went on their way,
and at dawn they arrived at the house. He started to pre-
pare coffee, and she in the meantime took off her shoes,
heard the crickets chirping, and thought happily that it
would soon be morning. Then they entered the bedroom.
A tongue of fire cut through the crown-of-thorns plants,
carbonized the dead horse slumped across the bed of yellow irises, and broke like an incandescent wave over the
guinea grass, which exploded into flame amidst the cack-
ling hens fluttering madly in fright; the flames kept spreading, they cut through the wire fence and reached the old
patch of wild pineapples, which instantly began to burn like
a long wick drenched in gasoline. The fire reached the cul-
tivated land, and the already yellowing cornfield trembled
with fury, vanishing in a dark glow. A few owls, blinded,
flew about in a frenzy, sometimes tumbling to the ground
where the circle of flame was mightiest. Old Rosa went on
crying in a measured flow, neither increasing nor decreas-
ing the intensity, paying no attention to the fire that occa-
sionally seemed to want to leap up to her hands. Nothing
happened the first night. Pablo took off his shirt, lay down

next to her, and ran his hands over her hips. She remained in her clothes, and when he went to take off his pants, she screamed. I'm tired, she said then, calmer; tomorrow will be different. He stopped unbuttoning his pants, sat down on the bed, grasped her hands, and pulling her to him, again lay down at her side. Rosa kept her eyes open and looked toward the rafters, which were lost in the darkness. And she wondered if it was not a sin in spite of everything, in spite of being married and in spite of the fact that the priest had blessed it. Holy Mother of God, she thought, maybe I just wasn't born for such things. With that she fell asleep. In the morning, Pablo woke her, bringing her a cup of coffee in bed. She stood up in her crumpled dress, took the coffee, and went out to the yard. Pablo went to her; very slowly he pressed against her from behind, slipping his hands over her breasts. You don't have a single saint in the bedroom, she said then, not looking at him. Tomorrow we're going to bring mine. As soon as night fell they retired. Rosa threw herself into bed, still in the dress she had worn all day, but Pablo, before she could protest, took off all his clothes and lay down naked at her side. For a long time the two of them were silent. Little by little she made out his face, his tousled hair falling over his eyes; then, hardly daring to breathe, she lowered her gaze and contemplated his hairy chest, his waist; and at last she brought herself to look down at his thighs, and there she lingered, terrified before that prominent muscle that rose, radiant, between the man's legs. Pablo did not speak; he lay face up with his hands crossed under his head, staring at the ceiling with unseeing eyes; and although several times he felt the desire to rip off her dress, he remained motionless, his erect organ bearing witness to the almost painful need to penetrate her. Thus they passed the night. But at dawn, he could stand it no longer, and almost crying, he pressed his face to Rosa's and started biting her with such fury that she was suddenly disconcerted. Animal, she said immediately. But he, infuriated, groped for the woman's body with his mouth, clutched her hips; finally he reached her knees and kissed her thighs and her feet. Animal, she kept repeating as she felt him panting over her body. And although she had to make a great effort not to cry out, she endured in silence. Afterward she resumed her chant, *Animal, animal,* but this time the words sounded far away and had a tone of resignation. The next day they did not get up; when it was growing dark, Pablo, in the spasms of a pleasure repeated beyond counting, heard the woman saying to him: *Tomorrow we're definitely going to get the saints.* They went. When they returned from the trip, the basket packed with plaster figures, portraits of virgins, silver crosses and hundreds of chains, medallions, and busts of virtually unknown martyrs and saints, Rosa began to set up a great altar in a corner of the bedroom. She spent the whole day arranging the figures, putting up long shelves to hold the largest images, nailing vases full of flowers to the beams; and when at last, in the afternoon, dripping with sweat, she completed the monumental installation, she threw herself on her knees and prayed for two hours. She asked, before all else, that the livestock multiply, that prosperity never abandon them; then she prayed for Pablo, that he stay strong. Oh, God, and don't let him grow old. Or me, God. And then her entreaty was not an entreaty but a kind of anguished protest. It was growing dark and still she had not completed her prayer. It was then that she sensed, or

almost imagined, the presence of a watchful shadow at her
back. She quickly looked behind her. But there was no one.
She was alone in the room. Sunlight filtered through the
window to the bed, bathing it in a pale glow that was
rapidly dissolving in the shadows. And suddenly she felt an
unfamiliar fear. And she left the room almost at a run.
Pablo, she said from the living room. Pablo, she said again
and again, and went out to the yard. There he was, carefully
closing the gate that led to the pasture. What's the matter,
he said to her, and pulled her to him. Nothing, she said.
And the two of them went into the house. It was completely dark, and Pablo lit the oil lamp.

Translated by Ann Tashi Slater and Andrew Hurley

The Lazarus Rumba

Ernesto Mestre

"I TOO HAVE KNOWN SORROW," doña Adela said to him as she let him into the parlor and took his thick-woven straw hat. She pressed her cheek to his and Father Gonzalo smelled her breath of desolation. She wore a loose printed housedress and slippers. Her hair was tied back in a tight bun so that the gray roots were accentuated and the many frizzled strands that had come loose set her face in a shadowy ruff apart from her small body, which moved in quick little bursts like a squirrel or a nervous child. Father Gonzalo followed a few steps behind her into the kitchen and doña Adela latched together the shuttered door and pushed open the window over the sink.

"Todo igual, coño. It's been two weeks and nothing has changed—all day locked in my room and wrapped in that musty old shawl she found the devil knows where. I think it was my mother's (la pobre, que en paz descanse). Y lo peor, now she has stopped eating altogether. She says the world smells too much of the dead and that it ruins her appetite. Imagínate, cosas de locos."

She searched the pockets of her printed housedress, till she came across a folded envelope, worn with handling.

She handed it to Father Gonzalo, informing him that the police captain had brought it to her the afternoon before. Father Gonzalo examined the contents of the envelope and shook his head and muttered that something had definitely gone awry when they could no longer properly bury their dead.

"A number. That is all the consolation we get for their murder . . . a number. 'For obvious reasons, and in the interest of national security, the revolutionary authorities reserve the right to bury its traitors.' Imagínate, when was that law passed? I have not shown it to her. I can't."

She offered him something to eat. Father Gonzalo shook his head. He was not hungry. "Un cafecito nada más, por favor, Adela. Then I'll go see her. Maybe she'll talk to me today. Maybe the fasting has awakened her spirit."

"She talks to no one except her cousin. He returned to town as soon as he heard what had happened. He spends hours with her. Pero no sé . . . how much good can he do when he is as faithless as a gypsy, behaves more like a child than she does."

"Adela, she is not a child. She is twenty-six."

"She is behaving like a child. She is not the first woman to lose a husband."

"Sí, verdad, Adela," Father Gonzalo shook the letter in his hand, "but the manner in which she lost him—"

"What about the manner in which I lost mine! You of all people know too well. It was enough to have buried myself with him, wrapped in a shroud of shame! But I endured (pues gracias a tí y a la Virgencita) and I will not have my daughter go mad. She too will endure. ¿No es así, Gonzalo? Won't she? Ay, no sé cuanto más puedo. Estoy completamente desesperada." She tried to hide her tears as she set the coffee down for her guest. Her hands had grown bonier and the veins were thick, bulging out like termite trails. Her fingernails were dull and bitten.

Father Gonzalo reached out and held her damp hands. He felt the sting of the cured mosquito bites on his back. "No seas boba, coño, you have to take care of yourself. Without you what will become of her? These days of doubt will nurture her faith when it grows again. La duda es pura mierda, Adela, but no other fertilizer can so richly nurture our faith."

Music came from Adela's room. Father Gonzalo recognized it and went silent and lowered his eyes and held a tight smile.

"Ay, esa música," doña Adela said, snatching her hands from his. "Como si esto fuera un manicomio. All day long with the same music and the stupid puzzles in that dark room where she can't even see at high day. I'm going to lose her, tan jovencita, mi única hija, and I'm going to lose . . . No! No! Coño, I won't lose her. I'll take that old shawl and the phonograph and all the scratched records and every piece of her silly jigsaws and build a bonfire in the patio, see what she does then!"

Father Gonzalo had his eyes closed and was listening with pleasure to the intruding melody. "You'd burn Beethoven?" he said, unable to sweeten the harsh tone of sanctimony.

"Que Dios me perdone, Gonzalo, but I'd burn Santa Victoria's handkerchief and Santa Teresa's heart a million times if it meant saving my daughter! What is it with her? I too have known sorrow. ¡Perdóname, Virgencita, perdóname!"

Father Gonzalo opened his eyes.

She now wept openly and folded her hands over her belly and finally her floating suffering face seemed to fuse into her body and her torso curled inward like the stalk of a rainstruck infant flower. From Adela's room, Beethoven's violin concerto reached a swollen pause. Father Gonzalo told Adela she had not done anything to deserve any of this. He told her that the Lord does not act like a scripted judge, meting out punishment for each sin.

"She is not the first," doña Adela said between sob-breaths. "The well of my patience is running dry, Gonzalo. Bien sabes, I too lost a husband."

A few days before the death of her husband, doña Adela had spoken the same words to Father Gonzalo. A director in a sugar mill, and then a renowned diplomat for the three elected governments before the 1952 coup d'état directed by the handsome Indian sergeant Fulgencio Batista, Teodoro Lucientes had been, in the eyes of the townsfolk in Guantánamo, a devoted father and a loving husband most of his life. Yet fate, as Father Gonzalo liked to say in his homilies, lives in a hovel near the foothills of tragedy. On the third week of his retired life (a career choice enforced by the new military regime that had many favors to dole out to those who helped undermine the elected governments) Teodoro suffered a coronary, and faced with such drastic evidence of his mortality, decided to turn his life inside-out, upside-down, blowing into the chasm of death, that is, ass-backward, so that he could face for the first time, in those few moments left, all those days, months, and years of shrouded desires. So Teodoro Lucientes's public life became his secret one, and his secret life his public one. (Indeed, his life had been no secret at all, for every thing that the eyes of the townsfolk of Guantánamo knew, their tongues, their blind tongues, knew two or three things better—and what tongue has never been stained with the ruby dye of gossip?) To put it plainly, sin pena ninguna, with the bluntness of the blindest, rubiest tongue, his wife and daughter became his mistress and bastard and his mistress and bastard became his wife and daughter.

After he returned from the hospital, he shuffled through the house wearing only a nightgown, his feet like giant eggplants. The doctors had prescribed that he move around the house and even take walks outside, but his ankles felt as if arrows were lodged there and he could not make it up and down the porch steps unless he had had a few drinks, which doña Adela (and the doctors) strictly forbade. One madrugada, after breaking the glass in the liquor cabinet and drinking half a bottle of rum, he discarded his nightgown and went out to the porch and swung on the blue porchswing, keeping rhythm as he stroked his semierect penis. The tender skin became chafed and bloody and he grew so tired that his forearms burned. He broke into tears, yearning for his other life. Shaken from her dream, in which she heard the screeches of the porchswing as the cries of a horde of hungry seagulls, doña Adela hurried outside and wrapped her husband in a colcha and cured him and guided him to bed, taping his penis to his stomach so that it would not stain the bedsheets. Teodoro, groggy with rum, looked at his organ distended with serous fluids. "Qué pena," he said, "so huge and so useless."

Doña Adela resisted the urge to slap him.

Two days later, after his siesta, Teodoro untaped his penis

and discarded the nightgown again, but this time he threw
on a wrinkled gray linen suit, and stuffed a blue-tongued
bird-of-paradise freshly plucked from his wife's garden into
the breast pocket and covered his rumpled mane of gray
with a stylish Panama and stiffened his sagging mustache
with labored curling motions and shuffled out to the terrace barefoot. He glanced only for a second at his wife sitting there, enjoying the afternoon breezes while rocking
herself on the rickety porchswing, in and out of her own
siesta.

"I am going to the sea," Teodoro said, his left eye flickering, "to walk in the sands of my youth."

Doña Adela could not muster up the strength to stop
him, though she knew he was not going anywhere near the
sea; and the first few times he did this, she regarded him
with an understanding and scrupulous pity, bemoaning to
anyone who might listen how her poor man had gone soft
in the head, loco loquito de la cabeza. Yet with each tiny
embarrassment of each afternoon departure, and with each
further humiliation on his return, sometimes way past dinnertime, six or seven hours later, sometimes way past the
following dinnertime, and the following, two or three days
later, rosy-faced and drunk with a long-deferred joy, pro-
claiming how wonderful and soothing the sea air was, her
pity began to break down like sugar in a still and ferment
into a harsh intolerance. At early Mass on Sundays, she
heard the ruby whispering behind her, and from the pulpit
Father Gonzalo noticed the tightening of her jaw muscles
as she whispered the Prayer of Contrition. One Sunday, she
approached Father Gonzalo outside the church, amid the
entire congregation, and pressed her lips so close to his ear

that they tickled him, and she whispered: "The well of my patience is running dry, Gonzalo. My husband is very ill. ¿A quién le rezo ahora? What kind of God listens to our prayers, anyway? What kind of God takes a man from his wife and lets him die in the bed of his whore?"

Because he had no answer to any of these questions, Father Gonzalo assured doña Adela that when the time came, Teodoro would die in her hands, but he warned her that it was a sin to so bluntly judge God by the manner in which He lets us stray from Him. Much better to judge Him, Father Gonzalo said, by the manner in which He guides us back toward His Bosom. Many years later, seated at her kitchen table, attempting to console her for the reclusive rebelliousness of her recently widowed daughter, he would use this very same logic, almost these very same words, though they had not proved very useful then and he doubted whether they would prove very useful this time. But it was the only way Father Gonzalo knew how to apply his faith, through a tenacious adherence to dictums that seemed to fly in the face of all common sense. But isn't that what faith is, the most uncommon sense?

And like all men of such uncommon sense, he had heavy doubts.

Why not judge God by the manner in which He lets us stray from Him? Would not any other father be judged by the way he turns from a wayward child, the rashness with which he shuts the front door of the house, then the kitchen door, then the servants' entrance, the conceit with which he stiffens his neck and covers his ears and sews tight his lips and draws the window shutters, so there is no passage through which grief can escape or the vanquished child can call to him, no passage through which he (the father) can answer? Isn't the manner in which He lets us stray, in fact, one and the same manner in which He calls us back? Is not His well-known silence God's greatest sin against His children? Sí, coño, for even the most benevolent father sins.

Why not Him?

Father Gonzalo knew that if Teodoro died in doña Adela's arms it would be mere chance, and completely against his will, such was the course of his madness, his inside-out last days, and the shameful details of these days that doña Adela whispered to Father Gonzalo and his servant Anita in the rectory kitchen after Mass on Sundays, they already knew. For who, even among the holy, can resist the ticklish prodding caresses of blind rubied tongues? How does a confessor interrupt a confession that has become a litany of another's sins?

Things were known.

On the eve of his retirement, Teodoro had bought for his mistress-that-was-now-like-his-wife a black Ford convertible, a thing so shiny with darkness that its too obviously symbolic color could be discerned better in the soft moonlight than in the garish sunlight. (It was the shame of the moon to be so enamored of this horrid machine that proved where no proof was needed Teodoro's infidelity—silky rays caressing its shiny coat, its leather seats, its buffed chrome, its glassy orbs, its dormant gauges. Le ronca, does the moon have nothing better on this earth to caress?) The thing—the yanqui machine—was conspicuously parked on the gravel, atop the hill, in front of the two-tiered olive house near the Bano River, the house that belonged to his mistress-that-was-now-like-his-wife's mother.

And her name? Or must the rubied tongues, out of sheer cowardice (for heaven forbid that their names ever be attached to their tongues), always speak this hyphen-happy slashy-sure anti-brevity margin-hugging speak? Her name for the soul of wit? (And these questions themselves asked without words, with the pursing of lips that first touch the hot cafecito, with a disquieting shift behind the confessional screen.)

Está bien . . . la Blanquita. That was her name, or at least that is what she was called.

That is all the rubied tongues offer for now; and with that, pursed lips and disquieting shifts are answered and they make do, and that they call her, as she was called: la Blanquita—she whose skin was veined and translucent as a yanqui's. Like rare Italian marble, some would say, or the face of the moon on a crisp blueblack night (in the ruby tales the moon is a crucial symbol, of light purloined, nature half-hidden). Like a varicose ankle, others claimed, or a rat fetus (dead, or better yet, unborn animals are also crucial symbols in these tales). Fine marble, a pretty moon. A tattooed ankle, a womb-plucked rat. A question of taste, or of situation.

Teodoro loved la Blanquita, and had loved her for many years, and had known her before he knew the woman he married, and about a year after impregnating his wife, impregnated her, so that his daughters numbered two, one aged fourteen, the other one almost thirteen, one named and called Alicia, the other one named one thing and called another—these two sisters almost strangers to each other, *almost* because Father Gonzalo knew that they sometimes—no, not sometimes, once a week exactly, on Tuesday afternoons—unknown to doña Adela, saw each other.

Things un-known were, claro (as is the nature of these tales), over-known.

Long before he had bought the black Ford convertible for la Blanquita, Teodoro had been extravagant in other ways, in ways the sun knew better than the moon. Under the pretext that a sister and a sister must know each other, every Tuesday afternoon he left early from his post at the mill and picked up his daughters at their separate schools and walked them hand in hand to the olive house on a hill near the Bano River. There, on the breezy veranda, they would enjoy the afternoon merienda with la Blanquita and her mother, who, when her daughter and her daughter's lover retired upstairs, entertained the sisters with wicked tales of demons and witches that lived among them. As time passed, Teodoro grew bolder and he would wander into town hand in hand with la Blanquita, flanked by his two daughters, and to those he ran into, at the barbershop, in the gardens of Parque Martí, at the movie theater, on the front steps of the yellow church, he would remain the gentleman he always was and lower his head and lift his Panama and greet with a simple "Pues buenas," and move on.

On Tuesday afternoons doña Adela had no husband, and for many years she let that be, taking her longest siestas on that day, and warning the servants, on pain of dismissal, that no one, for no reason, should raise his voice above a whisper, and much less disturb her, till her husband returned with her daughter from the beach, where they went each Tuesday afternoon. Only once was her long Tuesday siesta interrupted, and once proved enough. A young Indian girl, the daughter of one of the cooks, had snuck into the kitchen and, playing with the butcher knives, had sliced her hand open betwixt thumb and index finger and at the sight of her gushing blood began to wail, and neither her father nor the other servants, with cupped hands over her mouth and whispery consolations into her ears and kitchen rags around her hand, could get her to stop. Doña Adela appeared at the kitchen doorway, a long leather belt at her side, like a whip. The cook stepped away from his whimpering daughter as doña Adela approached, and he did nothing as he watched his employer beat his injured child with such venom that the rags came loose from her wounded hand and spread her blood in splashes all over, on the yellow walls, on the refrigerator doors, on the shiny countertops, on her father's apron, and on the dress and face of the woman who was so mercilessly administering uncounted lashes on his daughter's legs. When the beating was done, doña Adela, gasping for air, the drops of blood commingling with the sweat on her brow, told her cook that there was no need to worry, that he still had his job, and that he should get his poor daughter to a hospital. When Teodoro came home that evening, he diligently washed every drop of blood from the kitchen and that night did not sleep, re-covering the stained walls with a shiny coat of yellow. He never asked what had happened, and when the old cook tried to relate to him the story, he silenced him, assuring him that his gentle wife had never once laid a violent hand on her own daughter, much less on anybody else's daughter. And from then on, on the cook's daughter's birthday, year after year, Teodoro secretly gave her gifts as lavish and extravagant as the ones he gave Alicia on her own birthday.

With no other option, seemingly satisfied, the cook behaved as if the bright yellow walls had never been stained with his daughter's blood, and doña Adela was never again disturbed from her long Tuesday siesta, her patience long as Penelope's, till the day she approached Father Gonzalo and put her lips to his ear and asked him, befuddled as a three-year-old: "What kind of a God takes a man from his wife and lets him die in the bed of his whore?"

God, chided for His silence, answers Father Gonzalo.

When?

When He sees fit, when His servant is least in the mood for answers, most caught in the horridness of domesticity—in those crusty-eyed moments between dreams and the morning rays filtering through the mosquitero—there God is, too clever to come in dreams (that is only the stuff of stories), where his servant may defend himself with all the skill and wile of the beastly unconscious—for how often is He called to ease suffering, and He comes instead to prove that gouty joints are a mere inconvenience, a heresy, an affront to His imagination to say: "I am now at the worst. I am replete with morbid humors." For whosoever can mouth those words, the worst is yet to come.

Pero vaya, at least He answers. Digan lo que digan, He always returns His calls. Just that He is working in a different time scheme, and sometimes His servant forgets this, and unwarrantedly accuses Him of an unholy silence. His servant could not be more wrong. He is the chattiest god there ever was. All His servant has to do is open His Book and read the stories therein: the Lord answers!

He starts and ends with His most finished law, a law that no god before him dared conceive (much less put into practice), a law so revolutionary that it is the first law mock-revolutionaries cast aside. Did not Fidel, almost from the morning he rode into the capital—(Is that the Virgin on his breast? The glow of the tyrant on his cheeks?)—did not he cast it aside almost immediately?

God, chided for His silence, answers Father Gonzalo:

Every man's soul is his own, to it he answers before he answers to his Lord, so it must be; in his own heart he must fashion a likeness of that silent greatness. So it must be. Else the Lord go mad and the world be left Fatherless. What if a man begot twenty children and had to answer, under law, for each and all of their wrongs, and what if the children each begot twenty more and the man had to answer, under law, for all the wrongs of his children's children and, in time, for those of his children's children's children? Would there be any escape from damnation for this poor soul burdened by all his wrongful brood? So is the fate of your wretched Lord. Think of all My children, think of the awful generations of My brood. I am sick. Worse in being worshiped than you in worshiping. I can command the prayer's knee, but not that selfish heart that feels nothing beyond its own wringing, that with a set of woeful susurrations thinks he can, like a lazy tenant, transfer over the caring of his house to Me. Am I a handyman? Is that what your Lord has become: someone to tighten every leaky tearduct, unstop every clogged heart, straighten every crossed nerve, dig up every weed in the garden of your dreams, plug up every hole in the flesh of those houses I gave you, free of charge, a gift? And am I to be blamed when that house goes up in flames or is eaten by termites through your own negligence? No other creature is as ungrateful as My own children. And you have the gall to wonder why I so often go silent. Silence is my resting place. The only place in My own world where I find peace.

I am sick of this. Your house is your own. See to it, damn it!

On those days, Father Gonzalo listened to God cuss in a voice sophisticated and savage, understood and not understood as the cry of birds, not in his dreams (for as a sleeper he was almost dreamless) but during the course of the wakeful day; it passed through the holes of his tattered mosquitero as he rejoiced at the end of another sleepless night, wandered out from the sacristy as he most absently said morning Mass, buzzed along with the mosquitoes and black flies as he walked to the rectory to have his breakfast, creeped into his flesh when Anita did him spiders, burned at the tip of his one daily cigarette as he performed his egestions, flicked ashes at the urgings in his loins, cut in slivers of light through the brim of his straw hat as he daily visited the many in the parish who sought condolence, cuddled with him at the siesta hour, hissed from behind the voices of the few who came to afternoon confession, stewed in the okra broth Anita prepared for dinner, and then after dusk, just when Father Gonzalo's joints began their most honest ache, God abandoned him. He cursed no more. He went silent.

Not that He was not there, Father Gonzalo knew that God was always there, just that sometimes, like one in a dreamless sleep, or one who is replete with words but will not mouth them, He says nothing.

In the worst of his bedtime hours, when no position can bring comfort to his flaring joints, Father Gonzalo wonders if God dreams during the day, and if he, as his minister, somehow manages, unwittingly, to infiltrate himself into all of God's tempestuous nightmares.

What kind of God suffers more than those who pray to Him?

The Prophet

Luis Aguilar León

FROM A ROCK above the harbor, the Prophet studied the white sail of the ship that would return him to his homeland. A mixture of sadness and joy inundated his soul. For nine years, his wise and loving words had fallen on the population of Elmira. But as much as he loved these people, duty called him home. The hour of departure had come. He alleviated his melancholy with the thought that his durable teachings would fill the void of his absence.

As he stood there, a politician approached him. Master, he said, speak to us of the Cubans.

The Prophet gathered his white tunic in a fist and replied. "The Cubans live among you, but are not of you. Seek not to know them for their soul dwells in the impenetrable world of dualism. The Cubans drink happiness and bitterness from one cup. They make music from their tears and laugh to the music. The Cubans take jokes seriously and turn seriousness into a joke. And they don't know themselves.

"Never underestimate the Cubans. Saint Peter's right arm is a Cuban, and the Devil's best counselor is also Cuban. Cuba has yielded neither a saint nor an agnostic, yet the

Cubans sanctify among the heretics and heresize among the saints. Their spirit is universal and irreverent. The Cubans believe in the Catholic God, in Chango, in the lottery and the horoscope at the same time. They treat the gods like familiars and assail them when they fail to come through. They believe in no one and believe in everything. And they neither shed their illusions nor learn from delusions.

"Never argue with them. The Cubans are born with immense wisdom. They have no need to read, they know all. They need not travel, they have seen all. The Cubans are the Chosen People—chosen by themselves. And they pass through other peoples like a ghost over water.

"The Cubans can be characterized individually by sympathy and intelligence, in a group by yelling and passion. Every one of them carries the spark of genius, and geniuses do not mingle well. Consequently, reuniting Cubans is easy—uniting them impossible. A single Cuban can manage to gain everything in this world except for the applause of other Cubans.

"Speak not to them of logic. Logic implies reason and moderation, and Cubans are hyperbolic and immoderate. If you invite them to a restaurant, invite them not to the best restaurant in town but to the best restaurant in the world. When debating one, don't say, I disagree with you, say, You are totally and absolutely mistaken.

"They have a cannibalistic tendency. *Se la comió* (he ate it) is an expression of admiration. *Comerse un cable* (eating a cable) signifies a critical situation. And calling someone *comedor de excrementos* (excrement eater) is their most typical and lacerating insult. They are pyromaniacally inclined. *Ser la candela* (being a candle) means being the best. And they so love contradiction, they call beautiful women *mon-struos* (monsters) and erudites *bárbaros* (barbarians). And when asked for a favor, they don't say yes or no, rather Yes, why not.

"The Cubans intuit solutions before even knowing the problems. Actually, for them there is never a problem. They feel so superior, they call everyone *chico,* though they shrink before no one. If taken to some famous painter's studio, they will only say, I never got into painting myself. When they visit a doctor, they seldom ask what is wrong with them but explain what they know they have.

'They use diminutives like compliments, but also with the motive of diminishing the other. Thus, they ask for un *favorcito* (a little favor), offer a *tacita de café* (little cup of coffee), visit *por un ratico* (a little while), and accept *un pedacito* (a small bite) of dessert. Then again, the Cuban owner of a mansion celebrates his *casita* (little house), or the Mercedes car buyer his *carrito* (small car). They use nick-names with tender cruelty. For instance, they call pediatri-cians Herods, an unappealing person *cocktail de guisasos* (a spine-filled fruit cocktail), and an ineffective president *cuchara* (spoon) because he neither pinches nor cuts.

"When I visited their island, I admired their instanta-neous collective wisdom. Any single Cuban feels capable of defeating communism or capitalism, straightening out Latin America, eradicating hunger in Africa, and teach-ing the Germans philosophy. They forbid everyone from opining about Cuba while they generalize on the whole world; Chinese, Russians, Spaniards, and Eskimos in-cluded. And they balk that foreigners cannot grasp their simple and obvious formulas. So they live among you, and travel the earth, and can't understand why its peoples aren't like them."

The ship finished docking. Around the Prophet, the crowd gathered, clearly sad. The Prophet turned as if intending to speak, but emotion choked him. A long minute of palpable silence passed, suddenly broken by the ship's navigator with his unmistakable Cuban accent. "Decide, brother. Wrap up that bedsheet and climb aboard now. I'm behind schedule."

The Prophet turned once more to the crowd, made a gesture of resignation, and slowly boarded the ship.

We Came All the Way from Cuba So You Could Dress Like This?

Achy Obejas

I'M WEARING A GREEN SWEATER. It's made of some synthetic material, and it's mine. I've been wearing it for two days straight and have no plans to take it off right now.

I'm ten years old. I just got off the boat—or rather, the ship. The actual boat didn't make it: We got picked up halfway from Havana to Miami by a gigantic oil freighter to which they then tied our boat. That's how our boat got smashed to smithereens, its wooden planks breaking off like toothpicks against the ship's big metal hull. Everybody talks about American ingenuity, so I'm not sure why somebody didn't anticipate that would happen. But they didn't. So the boat that brought me and my parents most of the way from Cuba is now just part of the debris that'll wash up on tourist beaches all over the Caribbean.

As I speak, my parents are being interrogated by an official from the office of Immigration and Naturalization Services. It's all a formality because this is 1963, and no Cuban claiming political asylum actually gets turned away. We're evidence that the revolution has failed the middle class and that communism is bad. My parents—my father's an accountant and my mother's a social worker—are living, breathing examples of the suffering Cubans have endured under the tyranny of Fidel Castro.

The immigration officer, a fat Hungarian lady with sparkly hazel eyes and a perpetual smile, asks my parents why they came over, and my father, whose face is bright red from spending two days floating in a little boat on the Atlantic Ocean while secretly terrified, points to me—I'm sitting on a couch across the room, more bored than exhausted—and says, We came for her, so she could have a future.

The immigration officer speaks a halting Spanish, and with it she tells my parents about fleeing the Communists in Hungary. She says they took everything from her family, including a large country estate, with forty-four acres and two lakes, that's now being used as a vocational training center. Can you imagine that, she says. There's an official presidential portrait of John F. Kennedy behind her, which will need to be replaced in a week or so.

I fold my arms in front of my chest and across the green sweater. Tonight the U.S. government will put us up in a noisy transient hotel. We'll be allowed to stay there at tax-payer expense for a couple of days until my godfather—who lives with his mistress somewhere in Miami—comes to get us.

Leaning against the wall at the processing center, I notice a volunteer for Catholic Charities who approaches me with gifts: oatmeal cookies, a plastic doll with blond hair and a blue dress, and a rosary made of white plastic beads. She smiles and talks to me in incomprehensible English, speaking unnaturally loud.

My mother, who's watching while sitting nervously next to my father as we're being processed, will later tell me she remembers this moment as something poignant and good.

All I hold onto is the feel of the doll—cool and hard—and the fact that the Catholic volunteer is trying to get me to exchange my green sweater for a little gray flannel gym jacket with a hood and an American flag logo. I wrap myself up tighter in the sweater, which at this point still smells of salt and Cuban dirt and my grandmother's house, and the Catholic volunteer just squeezes my shoulder and leaves, thinking, I'm sure, that I've been traumatized by the trip across the choppy waters. My mother smiles weakly at me from across the room.

I'm still clutching the doll, a thing I'll never play with but which I'll carry with me all my life, from apartment to apartment, one move after the other. Eventually, her little blond nylon hairs will fall off and, thirty years later, after I'm diagnosed with cancer, she'll sit atop my dresser, scarred and bald like a chemo patient. . . .

Here's what my father dreams I will be in the United States of America: a lawyer, then a judge, in a system of law that is both serious and just. Not that he actually believes in democracy—in fact, he's openly suspicious of the popular will—but he longs for the power and prestige such a career would bring and which he can't achieve on his own now that we're here, so he projects it all on me. He sees me in courtrooms and lecture halls, at libraries and in elegant restaurants, the object of envy and awe.

My father does not envision me in domestic scenes. He does not imagine me as a wife or mother because to do so would be to imagine someone else closer to me than he is, and he cannot endure that. He will never regret not being a grandfather; it was never part of his plan.

Here's what my mother dreams I will be in the United States of America: the owner of many appliances and a rolling green lawn; mother of two mischievous children; the wife of a boyishly handsome North American man who drinks Pepsi for breakfast; a career woman with a well-paying position in local broadcasting.

My mother pictures me reading the news on TV at four and home at the dinner table by six. She does not propose that I will actually do the cooking, but rather that I'll oversee the undocumented Haitian woman my husband and I have hired for that purpose. She sees me as fulfilled as she imagines she is.

All I ever think about are kisses, not the deep throaty kind but quick pecks all along my belly just before my lover and I dissolve into warm blankets and tangled sheets in a bed under an open window. I have no view of this scene from a distance, so I don't know if the window frames tall pine trees or tropical bushes permeated with skittering gray lizards. . . .

My parents escaped from Cuba because they did not want me to grow up in a communist state. They are anti-communists, especially my father.

It's because of this that when Martin Luther King, Jr., dies in 1968 and North American cities go up in flames, my father will gloat. King was a Communist, he will say; he studied in Moscow, everybody knows that.

I'll roll my eyes and say nothing. My mother will ask him

to please finish his *café con leche* and wipe the milk mustache from the top of his lip.

Later, the morning after Bobby Kennedy's brains are shot all over a California hotel kitchen, my father will greet the news of his death by walking into our kitchen wearing a "Nixon's the One" button.

There's no stopping him now, my father will say; I know, because I was involved with the counterrevolution, and I know he's the one who's going to save us, he's the one who came up with the Bay of Pigs—which would have worked, all the experts agree, if he'd been elected instead of Kennedy, that coward.

My mother will vote for Richard Nixon in 1968, but in spite of his loud support my father will sit out the election, convinced there's no need to become a citizen of the United States (the usual prerequisite for voting) because Nixon will get us back to Cuba in no time, where my father's dormant citizenship will spring to life.

Later that summer, my father, who has resisted getting a television set (too cumbersome to be moved when we go back to Cuba, he will tell us), suddenly buys a huge Zenith color model to watch the Olympics broadcast from Mexico City.

I will sit on the floor, close enough to distinguish the different colored dots, while my father sits a few feet away in a LA-Z-BOY chair and roots for the Cuban boxers, especially Teófilo Stevenson. Every time Stevenson wins one—whether against North Americans or East Germans or whomever—my father will jump up and shout.

Later, when the Cuban flag waves at us during the medal ceremony, and the Cuban national anthem comes through the TV's tinny speakers, my father will stand up in Miami and cover his heart with his palm just like Fidel, watching on his own TV in Havana.

When I get older, I'll tell my father a rumor I heard that Stevenson, for all his heroics, practiced his best boxing moves on his wife, and my father will look at me like I'm crazy and say, Yeah, well, he's a Communist, what did you expect, huh?

In the processing center, my father is visited by a Cuban man with a large camera bag and a steno notebook into which he's constantly scribbling. The man has green Coke-bottle glasses and chews on a pungent Cuban cigar as he nods at everything my father says.

My mother, holding a brown paper bag filled with our new (used) clothes, sits next to me on the couch under the buzzing and clicking lights. She asks me about the Colombian girl, and I tell her she read me parts of the Bible, which makes my mother shudder.

The man with the Coke-bottle glasses and cigar tells my father he's from Santiago de Cuba in Oriente province, near Fidel's hometown, where he claims nobody ever supported the revolution because they knew the real Fidel. Then he tells my father he knew his father, which makes my father very nervous.

The whole northern coast of Havana harbor is mined, my father says to the Cuban man as if to distract him. There are *milicianos* all over the beaches, he goes on; it was a miracle we got out, but we had to do it—for her, and he points my way again.

Then the man with the Coke-bottle glasses and cigar

jumps up and pulls a giant camera out of his bag, covering my mother and me with a sudden explosion of light.

In 1971, I'll come home for Thanksgiving from Indiana University where I have a scholarship to study optometry. It'll be the first time in months I'll be without an antiwar demonstration to go to, a consciousness-raising group to attend, or a Gay Liberation meeting to lead.

Alaba'o, I almost didn't recognize you, my mother will say, pulling on the fringes of my suede jacket, promising to mend the holes in my floor-sweeping bell-bottom jeans. My green sweater will be somewhere in the closet of my bedroom in their house.

We left Cuba so you could dress like this? my father will ask over my mother's shoulder.

And for the first and only time in my life, I'll say, Look, you didn't come for me, you came for you; you came because all your rich clients were leaving, and you were going to wind up a cashier in your father's hardware store if you didn't leave, okay?

My father, who works in a bank now, will gasp—*¿Qué qué?*—and step back a bit. And my mother will say, Please, don't talk to your father like that.

And I'll say, It's a free country, I can do anything I want, remember? Christ, he only left because Fidel beat him in that stupid swimming race when they were little.

And then my father will reach over my mother's thin shoulders, grab me by the red bandanna around my neck, and throw me to the floor, where he'll kick me over and over until all I remember is my mother's voice pleading, Please stop, please, please, please stop.

We leave the processing center with the fat Hungarian lady, who drives a large Ford station wagon. My father sits in the front with her, and my mother and I sit in the back, although there is plenty of room for both of us in the front as well. The fat Hungarian lady is taking us to our hotel, where our room will have a kitchenette and a view of an alley from which a tall black transvestite plies her night trade.

Eventually, I'm drawn by the lights of the city, not just the neon streaming by the car windows but also the white globes on the street lamps, and I scamper to the back where I can watch the lights by myself. I close my eyes tight, then open them, loving the tracers and star bursts on my private screen.

Up in front, the fat Hungarian lady and my father are discussing the United States' many betrayals, first of Eastern Europe after World War II, then of Cuba after the Bay of Pigs invasion.

My mother, whom I believe is as beautiful as any of the palm trees fluttering on the median strip as we drive by, leans her head against the car window, tired and bereft. She comes to when the fat Hungarian lady, in a fit of giggles, breaks from the road and into the parking lot of a supermarket so shrouded in light that I'm sure it's a flying saucer docked here in Miami.

We did this when we first came to America, the fat Hungarian lady says, leading us up to the supermarket. And it's something only people like us can appreciate.

My father bobs his head up and down and my mother follows, her feet scraping the ground as she drags me by the hand.

We walk through the front door and then a turnstile, and suddenly we are in the land of plenty—row upon row of cereal boxes, TV dinners, massive displays of fresh pineapple, crate after crate of oranges, shelves of insect repellent, and every kind of broom. The dairy section is jammed with cheese and chocolate milk.

There's a butcher shop in the back, and my father says, Oh my god, look, and points to a slab of bloody red ribs thick with meat. My god my god my god, he says, as if he's never seen such a thing, or as if we're on the verge of starvation.

Calm down, please, my mother says, but he's not listening, choking back tears and hanging off the fat Hungarian lady who's now walking him past the sausages and hot dogs, packaged bologna and chipped beef.

All around us people stare, but then my father says, We just arrived from Cuba, and there's so much here!

The fat Hungarian lady pats his shoulder and says to the gathering crowd, Yes, he came on a little boat with his whole family; look at his beautiful daughter who will now grow up well fed and free.

I push up against my mother, who feels as smooth and thin as a palm leaf on Good Friday. My father beams at me, tears in his eyes. All the while, complete strangers congratulate him on his wisdom and courage, give him hugs and money, and welcome him to the United States.

There are things that can't be told.

Things like when we couldn't find an apartment, everyone's saying it was because landlords in Miami didn't rent to families with kids, but knowing, always, that it was more than that.

Things like my doing very poorly on an IQ test because I didn't speak English, and getting tossed into a special education track, where it took until high school before somebody realized I didn't belong there.

Things like a North American hairdresser's telling my mother she didn't do her kind of hair.

Like my father, finally realizing he wasn't going to go back to Cuba anytime soon, trying to hang himself with the light cord in the bathroom while my mother cleaned rooms at a nearby luxury hotel, but falling instead and breaking his arm.

Like accepting welfare checks, because there really was no other way.

Like knowing that giving money to exile groups often meant helping somebody buy a private yacht for Caribbean vacations, not for invading Cuba, but also knowing that refusing to donate only invited questions about our own patriotism.

And knowing that Nixon really wasn't the one, and wasn't doing anything, and wouldn't have done anything, even if he'd finished his second term, no matter what a good job the Cuban burglars might have done at the Watergate Hotel.

What if we'd stayed? What if we'd never left Cuba? What if we were there when the last of the counterrevolution was beaten, or when Mariel harbor leaked thousands of Cubans out of the island, or when the Pan-American Games came? What if we'd never left?

All my life, my father will say I would have been a young Communist, falling prey to the revolution's propaganda. According to him, I would have believed ice cream treats came from Fidel, that those hairless Russians were our friends, and that my duty as a revolutionary was to turn him in for his counterrevolutionary activities—which he will swear he'd never have given up if we'd stayed in Cuba.

My mother will shake her head but won't contradict him. She'll say the revolution uses people, and that I, too, would probably have been used, then betrayed, and that we'll never know, but maybe I would have wound up in jail whether I ever believed in the revolution or not, because I would have talked back to the wrong person, me and my big mouth.

I wonder, if we'd stayed then who, if anyone—if not Martha and the boy from the military academy—would have been my blond lovers, or any kind of lovers at all.

And what if we'd stayed, and there had been no revolution?

My parents will never say, as if somehow they know that their lives were meant to exist only in opposition.

I try to imagine who I would have been if Fidel had never come into Havana sitting triumphantly on top of that tank, but I can't. I can only think of variations of who I am, not who I might have been.

In college one day, I'll tell my mother on the phone that I want to go back to Cuba to see, to consider all these questions, and she'll pause, then say, What for? There's nothing there for you, we'll tell you whatever you need to know, don't you trust us?

Over my dead body, my father will say, listening in on the other line.

Years later, when I fly to Washington, D.C., and take a cab straight to the Cuban Interests Section to apply for a visa, a golden-skinned man with the dulled eyes of a bureaucrat will tell me that because I came to the U.S. too young to make the decision to leave for myself—that it was in fact my parents who made it for me—the Cuban government does not recognize my U.S. citizenship.

You need to renew your Cuban passport, he will say. Perhaps your parents have it, or a copy of your birth certificate, or maybe you have a relative or friend who could go through the records in Cuba for you.

I'll remember the passport among my mother's priceless papers, handwritten in blue ink, even the official parts. But when I ask my parents for it, my mother will say nothing, and my father will say, It's not here anymore, but in a bank box, where you'll never see it. Do you think I would let you betray us like that? . . .

When my father dies of a heart attack in 1990 (it will happen while he's driving, yelling at somebody, and the car will just sail over to the sidewalk and stop dead at the curb, where he'll fall to the seat and his arms will somehow fold over his chest, his hands set in prayer), I will come home to Florida from Chicago, where I'll be working as a photographer for the *Tribune*. I won't be taking pictures of murder scenes or politicians then but rather rock stars and local performance artists.

I'll be living in Uptown, in a huge house with a dry darkroom in one of the bedrooms, now converted and sealed black, where I cut up negatives and create photomontages that are exhibited at the Whitney Biennial and hailed by the critics as filled with yearning and hope.

When my father dies, I will feel sadness and a wish that certain things had been said, but I will not want more time with him. I will worry about my mother, just like all the relatives who predict she will die of heartbreak within months (she has diabetes and her vision is failing). But she will instead outlive both him and me.

I'll get to Miami Beach, where they've lived in a little coach house off Collins Avenue since their retirement, and find cousins and aunts helping my mother go through insurance papers and bank records, my father's will, his photographs and mementos: his university degree, a faded list of things to take back to Cuba (including Christmas lights), a jaundiced clipping from *Diario de las Américas* about our arrival which quotes my father as saying that Havana harbor is mined, and a photo of my mother and me, wide-eyed and thin, sitting on the couch in the processing center. . . .

There will be a storm during my father's burial, which means it will end quickly. My mother and several relatives will go back to her house, where a TV will blare from the bedroom filled with bored teenage cousins, the women will talk about how to make *picadillo* with low-fat ground turkey instead of the traditional beef and ham, and the men will sit outside in the yard, drinking beer or small cups of Cuban coffee, and talk about my father's love of Cuba, and how unfortunate it is that he died just as Eastern Europe is breaking free, and Fidel is surely about to fall.

Three days later, after taking my mother to the movies and the mall, church and the local Social Security office, I'll be standing at the front gate with my bags, yelling at the cab driver that I'm coming, when my mother will ask me to wait a minute and run back into the house, emerging minutes later with a box for me that won't fit in any of my bags.

A few things, she'll say, a few things that belong to you that I've been meaning to give you for years and now, well, they're yours.

I'll shake the box, which will emit only a muffled sound, and thank her for whatever it is, hug her and kiss her and tell her I'll call her as soon as I get home. She'll put her chicken bone arms around my neck, kiss the skin there all the way to my shoulders, and get choked up, which will break my heart.

Sleepy and tired in the cab to the airport, I'll lean my head against the window and stare out at the lanky palm trees, their brown and green leaves waving goodbye to me through the still coming drizzle. Everything will be damp, and I'll be hot and stuffy, listening to car horns detonating on every side of me. I'll close my eyes, stare at the blackness, and try to imagine something of yearning and hope, but I'll fall asleep instead, waking only when the driver tells me we've arrived, and that he'll get my bags from the trunk, his hand outstretched for the tip as if it were a condition for the return of my things.

When I get home to Uptown I'll forget all about my mother's box until one day many months later when my memory's fuzzy enough to let me be curious. I'll break it open to find grade school report cards, family pictures of the three of us in Cuba, a love letter to her from my father (in which he talks about wanting to kiss the tender mole by her mouth), Xeroxes of my birth certificate, copies of our requests for political asylum, and my faded blue-ink Cuban passport (expiration date: June 1965), all wrapped up in my old green sweater.

When I call my mother—embarrassed about taking so

long to unpack her box, overwhelmed by the treasures within it—her answering machine will pick up and, in a bilingual message, give out her beeper number in case of emergency.

A week after my father's death, my mother will buy a computer with a Braille keyboard and a speaker, start learning how to use it at the community center down the block, and be busy investing in mutual funds at a profit within six months.

But this is all a long way off, of course. Right now, we're in a small hotel room with a kitchenette that U.S. taxpayers have provided for us.

My mother, whose eyes are dark and sunken, sits at a little table eating one of the Royal Castle hamburgers the fat Hungarian lady bought for us. My father munches on another, napkins spread under his hands. Their heads are tilted toward the window which faces an alley. To the far south edge, it offers a view of Biscayne Boulevard and a magically colored thread of night traffic. The air is salty and familiar, the moon brilliant hanging in the sky.

I'm in bed, under sheets that feel heavy with humidity and the smell of cleaning agents. The plastic doll the Catholic volunteer gave me sits on my pillow.

Then my father reaches across the table to my mother and says, We made it, we really made it.

And my mother runs her fingers through his hair and nods, and they both start crying, quietly but heartily, holding and stroking each other as if they are all they have.

And then there's a noise—a screech out in the alley followed by what sounds like a hyena's laughter—and my father leaps up and looks out the window, then starts laughing, too.

Oh my god, come here, look at this, he beckons to my mother, who jumps up and goes to him, positioning herself right under the crook of his arm. Can you believe that, he says.

Only in America, echoes my mother.

And as I lie here wondering about the spectacle outside the window and the new world that awaits us on this and every night of the rest of our lives, even I know we've already come a long way. What none of us can measure yet is how much of the voyage is already behind us.

Contributors

ANN LOUISE BARDACH is the author of the forthcoming book *Cuba Confidential* (Random House). She
has written extensively about Cuba for the *New York
Times*, *Talk*, *Vanity Fair*, *Condé Nast Traveler*, the *New Re-
public*, the *Washington Post*, and other publications.

∽

LUIS AGUILAR LEÓN (1925–) was born and raised in
Oriente, Cuba. He attended the Jesuit-run Dolores grade
school with Fidel Castro. A professor of Cuban history,
he has taught at Oriente University, Columbia, Cornell,
and Georgetown and has written several books of both
essays and fiction. He defines himself as a "skeptical
humanist."

MARÍA EUGENIA ALEGRÍA NUÑEZ (1953–) is
a critic and translator, and has published a collection
of short stories in Cuba. She is a member of the edi-
torial collective *Vigía*, based in Matanzas and lives in
Varadero.

UVA DE ARAGÓN (1944–) came to the States in 1959. She has written nine books including two short story collections, poetry, essays, and *Alfonso Hernández Catá: Un escritor cubano, salmantino y universal* (1996), a critical essay on the Cuban novelist and short-story writer who was her maternal grandfather. Uva de Aragón is Associate Director of the Cuban Research Institute at Florida International University and Associate Editor of *Cuban Studies*, an academic journal. She writes a weekly column for *Diario las Américas*.

REINALDO ARENAS (1943–1990) came from an impoverished and uneducated family from Holguín, Cuba. He studied at the University of Havana and was later mentored by José Lezama Lima. After a protracted period where he was ostracized and imprisoned, he fled with the 1980 Mariel exodus. In the United States he co-founded and edited the cultural magazine *Mariel* (1983–1985). Arenas authored seven novels, five novelas, collections of short stories, essays, experimental theater pieces, and poetry. Dying of AIDS, he took his life in 1990. His posthumously published memoir, *Before Night Falls*, was made into a film in 2000.

RICHARD BLANCO (1960–) was made in Cuba, assembled in Spain, and imported to the United States, he says, meaning that his seven-month pregnant mother and the rest of the family arrived as exiles from Cienfuegos, Cuba, to Madrid, where he was born, then moved to the States. His work has appeared in *The Nation, Indiana Review, Michigan Quarterly,* and *Tri-quarterly Review*.

LINO NOVÁS CALVO (1905–1983) was born in Spain and came to Cuba with his family in 1912. He worked as a caterer from a young age to support himself and later moved on to journalism. As a foreign correspondent he covered the Spanish Civil War from 1931 to 1936. On his return to Havana, he taught French and continued to write short stories and translated Hemingway, Faulkner, Huxley, and others into Spanish. In 1942 he won the Hernández Catá Prize for the story *Un dedo encima*. In 1960 he sought asylum in the Colombian Embassy. In exile, he taught at the University of Syracuse and continued to write until his death.

CALVERT CASEY (1924–1969) was the son of an American father and Cuban mother, who had moved to Cuba as a teenager. One of his first short stories, *El Paseo*, published in the *New Mexico Quarterly,* won a prize from Doubleday. With the advent of the Revolution, he joined the new wave of writers and intellectuals and wrote for several publications, including reviews for the celebrated *Lunes de revolución.* His anthology of short stories, *El Regreso* (Barcelona, 1962) was followed by *Memorias de una isla*, a collection of articles on Cuban culture. He left Cuba in 1966. Three years later, he committed suicide in Rome.

ALFONSO HERNÁNDEZ CATÁ (1885–1940) belonged to the first generation of Cuban writers and was a master of every literary genre. Considered one of the fathers of Cuba's short story, his stories follow the tradition of Poe and Maupassant and are known for their psychological insights and modernist style. He is known for his treatment and foresight in such themes as racism (*La Piel*, 1923), homosexuality (*El Angel de sodoma*, 1929), and dictatorship (*Un Cementerio en la Antillas*, 1933). Hernández Catá also served as Cuba's ambassador to Brazil where he died in an airplane crash.

JOSEFINA DE DIEGO (1951–) was born into a Cuban literary family; her father was the noted writer Eliseo Diego. She lives in Havana where she is an economist by profession. Her first book of stories, *Grandfather's Kingdom*, was published in Mexico in 1993.

ABILIO ESTÉVEZ (1954–) was born in Havana, where he still resides. He was mentored by the Cuban master Virgilio Piñera and has written several plays, including the award-winning *Night*; a collection of poems, *Manuel of Temptations*; a volume of short stories, *Game with Gloria*; and essays.

LEONARDO PADURA FUENTES (1955–) is an essayist, journalist, and novelist. He has written a quartet of detective novels, of which *Máscaras,* excerpted here, is the third. All of the novels are set in Havana and revolve around the travails of detective Lt. Mario Conde. He won the 1993 Premio UNEAC for his novel *Vientos de Cuaresma*. He lives in Havana.

CRISTINA GARCIA (1958–) was born in Havana, Cuba, and grew up in New York City. She attended Barnard College and Johns Hopkins University, and worked as a correspondent for *Time* magazine. She has published two widely acclaimed novels, *Dreaming in Cuban* and *The Agüero Sisters*. Her third novel, *Monkey Hunting,* is forthcoming.

PEDRO JUAN GUTIÉRREZ (1950–) began working life at the age of eleven as an ice cream vendor and newsboy. Formerly a journalist, he lives in Havana, devoting himself to writing and painting. The author of several volumes of poetry, Gutiérrez's first novel was *El Rey de la Habana.*

JOSÉ LEZAMA LIMA (1910–1976) is regarded as one of Cuba's foremost writers, best known for his Proustian masterpiece, *Paradiso* (1966). He is also the author of short stories, essays, poetry, and translations of French literature. With José Rodríguez Feo, he created the Cuban literary journal *Origenes,* which published and celebrated the work of the most original writers and artists in Cuba. After graduating law school, he worked at the Ministry of Culture from 1945 to 1950. After the Revolution, he was gradually sidelined because of his homosexuality and the eroticism of his work. Today, however, he is widely celebrated as Cuba's foremost modern writer and his Vedado home has been restored as a museum.

PABLO MEDINA (1948–) was born in Cuba and came to the United States with his family as a child. A graduate in English and Spanish literature from Georgetown University, Medina is the author of three published collections of poetry, *Pork Rind and Cuban Songs* (1975), *Arching into the Afterlife* (1991), and *The Floating Island* (1999); two novels, *Marks of Birth* (1994), *The Return of Felix Nogara* (2000); and a memoir, *Exiled Memories: A Cuban Childhood* (1990).

ANA MENÉNDEZ (1970–) was born in Los Angeles to exile parents and later moved to Miami. She is the author of a collection of short stories entitled *In Cuba I Was a German Shepherd*. As a reporter, she worked for the *Orange County Register* and the *Miami Herald*.

ERNESTO MESTRE (1964–) was born in Guantanamo, Cuba, and left for Madrid in 1972 with his family and soon after settled in Miami. He graduated from Tulane University and taught at Sarah Lawrence College. He lives in Brooklyn, New York.

MAYRA MONTERO (1952–) was born in Havana and now lives in Puerto Rico. She has written four highly acclaimed novels and a collection of stories in Spanish. Her two most recent novels, *In the Palm of Darkness* and *The Messenger*, have appeared in English translation, along with an earlier novel, *The Last Night I Spent with You*.

ACHY OBEJAS (1956–) came to the United States at the age of six and now lives in Chicago where she is a columnist at the *Chicago Tribune*. She is the author of two novels, *Days of Awe* (Ballantine, 2001) and *Memory Mambo* (1996), and has published her poetry in various U.S. magazines.

SENEL PAZ (1950–) grew up in the countryside of Las Villas, Cuba. On a scholarship after the Revolution, he was sent to Havana to pursue his education where he graduated with distinction. He was mentored by the writer, Eduardo Heras León, who was later accused of writing antirevolutionary stories. His novella, *The Wolf, the Woods and the New Man*, won the Juan Rulfo Prize awarded by Radio France International in 1990, and was adapted by Paz into the screenplay for the Academy Award–nominated film *Strawberry and Chocolate*, directed by the late Tomas Gutiérrez Alea. He lives in Havana.

ANTONIO JOSÉ PONTE (1964–) was born in 1964 in Matanzas, Cuba. In 1980, he moved to Havana, where he attended and graduated from the University of Havana. After five years working as an engineer in rural eastern Cuba, he became a screenwriter and filmmaker, before moving into literature. Ponte has published three books of poetry, essays, novels, and short stories.

ZOÉ VALDÉS (1959–) was born in Havana. She is a poet, novelist, and short-story writer. She worked for years at the Cuban Film Institute and was later a member of the Cuban delegation at UNESCO in Paris, where she now lives with her daughter. Her novel *La Nada Cotidiana* was a finalist for the 1996 Planeta Prize in Spain, and was published in the United States as *Yocandra in the Paradise of Nada*. She is also the author of *I Gave You All I Had*, published by Arcade.

~

TRANSLATORS

Peter Bush	John H. R. Polt
Sabina Cienfuegos	Barbara Paschke
Dick Cluster	Gregory Rabassa
Lisa Davis	Raymond Sayers
Cola Franzen	Ann Tashi Slater
David Frye	and Andrew Hurley
Edith Grossman	Natasha Wimmer

We wish to gratefully acknowledge the superb contribution of all the translators in this collection. We do not have the space to include biographical information for them here, but it can be found at our website:

www.whereaboutspress.com

CPSIA information can be obtained
at www.ICGtesting.com
Printed in the USA
LVOW10n1708120418
573021LV00009B/5/P